REBOUND CAPER

"*What . . . is . . . that?*"

The words came as individual shouts, each separated from the other by a long pause.

The Pirates, first on the court, were a couple of minutes into their warm-up s̶ the Bennington Falcons walke̶ ake the court. Gary h̶ iforms out of the corn̶ n the impulse to tu̶ ing, he raced under the ̶ off a rebound.

But now he h̶ ̶houted, "*What . . . is . . . that?*" He turned. And saw a woman, lanky, with short-cropped blond hair, wearing slacks and a blue sweatshirt with *Falcons* printed on the front. Beyond her, a group of girls in blue uniforms with silver trim stood motionless. They were looking at him. Gary had never seen the woman before. She was pointing at him—and looking at the Pirates' coach, Monica Conway, who was now walking across the court to meet her.

"*Is . . . that . . . a . . . boy?*"

Gary turned to his teammates. "I think she might be talking about me," he said, grinning.

"Fast-paced and involving."
—*School Library Journal*

PUFFIN BOOKS BY THOMAS J. DYGARD

THOMAS J. DYGARD

Rebound Caper

PUFFIN BOOKS

PUFFIN BOOKS
Published by the Penguin Group
Viking Penguin, a division of Penguin Books USA Inc.,
375 Hudson Street, New York, New York 10014, U.S.A.
Penguin Books Ltd, 27 Wrights Lane, London W8 5TZ, England
Penguin Books Australia Ltd, Ringwood, Victoria, Australia
Penguin Books Canada Ltd, 10 Alcorn Avenue, Toronto, Ontario, Canada M4V 3B2
Penguin Books (N.Z.) Ltd, 182–190 Wairau Road, Auckland 10, New Zealand

Penguin Books Ltd, Registered Offices: Harmondsworth, Middlesex, England

First published in the United States of America
by William Morrow and Company, Inc., 1983
Reprinted by arrangement with William Morrow and Company, Inc.
Published in Puffin Books, 1992
3 5 7 9 10 8 6 4 2

LIBRARY OF CONGRESS CATALOGING-IN-PUBLICATION DATA
Dygard, Thomas J.
Rebound caper / by Thomas Dygard.   p.   cm.
Summary: High-school basketball player Gary Whipple, known for his
mischievous pranks, creates a sensation when he switches from the
boys' team to the girls' team.
ISBN 0-14-034913-8
[1. Basketball—Fiction.   2. Schools—Fiction.]   I. Title.
[PZ7.D9893Re 1992]   [Fic]—dc20   91-31470

Printed in the United States of America
Set in Caledonia

FOR MY PARENTS

Rebound
Caper

Chapter One

If any boy in the history of Madison High was going to quit the boys' basketball team and go out for the girls' team, Gary Whipple was sure to be the one.

The night of the junior prom the previous spring, when Gary—fully clothed in a new suit, with a flower between his teeth—swan-dived off the second-floor railing of the Holiday Inn into the swimming pool, nobody had to ask who made the splash. They knew it was Gary Whipple.

When the odor of rotten eggs wafted through the chemistry lab and out into the corridors of Madison High, Miss Griffin did not have to look around to discover who had successfully mastered the manufacture of hydrogen sulfide. She marched straight to the lab table where Gary Whipple was working.

When laughter instead of cheers echoed beyond the walls of the Madison High gymnasium during a basketball game, nobody had to ask who was at it again. They knew it was Gary Whipple. He was dribbling on his knees, which always brought a roar from the crowd and left opponents staring in slack-jawed disbelief. Or he was faking a sudden throw into the face of an opponent guarding him. The startled guard would almost jump out of his skin, and the crowd always laughed. Or Gary was snapping to attention and delivering a crisp military salute to a teammate—or even an opponent—in recognition of an outstanding play. The crowd always roared.

For the Madison High fans in the basketball hotbed of northern Illinois, the antics of Gary Whipple were a bonus attraction on game night. From his chemistry classmates, even while the foul odor was in their nostrils, the prank provoked giggles and grins. Indeed, Miss Griffin seemed alone in failing to appreciate the gag. As for the witnesses to the Holiday Inn swan dive, they still were talking about it.

Gary Whipple, more than anyone, enjoyed center stage.

All the same, everyone was surprised when Gary abruptly quit the boys' basketball team and signed up for the girls' team.

Coach Orville Flynn, the guiding hand of the Madison High Pirates for more than twenty-five years, unwittingly set in motion the chain of events that led Gary into the lineup of the girls' team.

Courtly, balding, with a rotundity that belied his background as a great college player in his youth, Orville Flynn led his teams with a gentle hand. He called his players "my boys." He addressed them as "son." He never raised his voice in anger. Orville Flynn was a formal man, always wearing a suit and tie to the Pirates' games. His attire conveyed to his players the message that he considered a Pirates basketball game an event worthy of a certain degree of dignity. Nobody, neither players nor fans, called him

Coach Flynn. They called him Mr. Flynn. At Madison High, they always had. It was befitting the manner and demeanor of the man.

Everyone in Madison always assumed that Orville Flynn was hiding a tough streak behind the kindly exterior. He never had to act tough. He achieved his desired results by inspiring, teaching, and by understanding the problems of his players. But everyone always figured that the toughness was there, carefully veiled.

The fans attending the third game of the season had no way of knowing they were about to witness an example of Mr. Flynn's smoothly disguised toughness, and the generation of a historic moment for Madison High.

The Pirates, winners of their first two games in the young season, were rolling over the outgunned Ridgeway Panthers with ease. In the early moments of the third quarter, the Pirates held a fourteen-point lead. Already, Orville Flynn was sending in his substitutes.

One of the substitutes was Gary Whipple. A senior, Gary had twice gained a letter, but never had cracked the starting lineup. The competition for the starting slots was fierce. The tradition of winning at Madison High had created intense interest in basketball all the way down into the kindergarten level. The result was a steady stream of talented, mature players. Among them, Gary was a skillful dribbler—how else could he dribble on his knees?—and an above-average shooter. But he was not unusually tall, standing five feet, eleven inches. Nor was he unusually strong, weighing only one hundred and sixty pounds. In the final totaling up, others always won the starting slot ahead of him. Gary began each game sitting on the bench.

Some said—and Orville Flynn was one of them—that Gary lacked the dedication to thrust himself into a starting role. Gary's answer—to himself, not to Mr. Flynn—was simple: he would rather have fun. Whatever the reasons, Gary Whipple was the sixth or seventh player on the team, never a starter, but one who always saw a lot of game action.

At this particular moment in the third quarter the action was at the edge of the keyhole in front of the Ridgeway goal. A Ridgeway player had just intercepted a pass. He dribbled twice and then stopped. He looked for a teammate to take a pass. Then, all of a sudden, he did not have the ball. Gary, coming around from behind the Ridgeway player, lifted the ball out of his hands and dribbled away. Keeping the ball, Gary dribbled inside the free-throw line. He jumped and fired for the basket. The ball soared over the outstretched hands of the Ridgeway center and dropped through the hoop.

The play was a nifty one, no question about it. And the Madison High fans, enjoying themselves in the Pirates' runaway victory, gave Gary a big cheer.

As the ball dropped through the net, Gary circled under the basket, trotted back out to the edge of the keyhole, and took a bow, beaming and waving to the crowd all the while. And not one bow, but two—first to the fans in the bleachers on one side of the gymnasium, then a stiff military about-face, and a bow to the fans in the other bleachers.

The fans, still on their feet to cheer the scoring

4

play, roared with laughter at the first deep bow. The laughter swelled in a crescendo as Gary executed the about-face and gave the second low bow. Then it gave way to a round of applause.

At the far end of the court Gary's teammates, taking up their defensive positions, watched. Gary's friend Howie Fenton was grinning broadly in appreciation of Gary's act. The two guards, Leon Bowman and Tim O'Reagan, smiled with a vague sort of tolerance. They had seen it before. The center, Horse Mueller, glowered his disapproval.

At the near end of the court the two Ridgeway guards, preparing to bring the ball back inbounds to resume play, were gaping in wonder.

In the crowd of cheerleaders at the sideline, Kimberly Bennett, Gary's steady girl friend of more than a year, was doubled over, her face buried in her hands, feigning horrible embarrassment. But Gary knew better. Behind the spread-out fingers of both hands, Kimberly Bennett was laughing. Kimberly always laughed at Gary's gags.

And at the Pirates' bench, as calmly as if he were flicking a piece of lint off his coat sleeve, Orville Flynn ordered Gary off the court and placed him on the bench, where he remained the rest of the game.

After the game, in the dressing room, Gary knew what to expect. First, Howie Fenton was going to be laughing and proclaiming the whole scene to be a real scream. Next, Horse Mueller, whom the teachers called Harold, was going to be frowning a lot. Horse was like that. Horse took everything, even the game of basketball, very seriously.

Of the other players, some would giggle with

Howie. Raymo Bailey, the starting forward with Howie, always enjoyed a good laugh. So did Hubie Thompson, a second-stringer. Leon, a starting guard, and Tim, a substitute guard, might smile but would never join in the general hilarity around Gary.

In the end, Mr. Flynn was sure to drop by Gary's locker just as Gary was buckling his trousers or tying his shoes, and he would say, "Son, let me see you a minute before you leave."

Beyond Mr. Flynn, Gary would be able to see the face of Mike Moseley, the assistant coach, watching. Mike Moseley did not approve of Gary's antics.

Then, a few minutes later, in a corner of the empty dressing room, Mr. Flynn would say, "Son, that was poor behavior. It reflected badly on the team. You must learn to discipline yourself."

And Gary would grin and shrug and leave the gymnasium.

Gary knew the scenario by heart. He had been through it half a dozen times. First, as a sophomore, when he dribbled on his knees the first time. The game had been a runaway, so what was there to lose? Nothing. And what was there to gain? Well, it was fun—for Gary, for his teammates, for the crowd. So who cared? Mr. Flynn cared, for one. Gary had sat out the rest of that game, and in the dressing room later, heard the first of the monologues he was to come to know so well. Last year, as a junior, there were the salutes, the fake passes in the faces of opponents, another knee-dribbling act. And always a quick trip to the bench, with the laughter of the crowd ringing in his ears, and after the game a short lecture in a corner of the dressing room. This year, at the start of practice, Mr. Flynn had given Gary a questioning look. He seemed ready to say, "You're a senior now, so act like one." But Mr. Flynn said nothing. Neither did Gary.

So Gary knew what was coming as he tied his shoe and spotted Mr. Flynn moving across the dressing room toward him.

Gary sensed something different in the wind when Mr. Flynn brought Mike Moseley to join their meeting. Always before, the assistant coach was left a distance away while Mr. Flynn, fatherly and friendly, explained the wrongs of Gary's ways. But there was Mike Moseley, coming along behind Mr. Flynn, as if he were part of whatever was going to happen. The atmosphere this time was definitely more ominous.

"Son, it hurts me to do this," Mr. Flynn said, "but I am benching you until further notice." He spoke the words in the quiet, comforting, reassuring tones of a geometry teacher telling a confused student that only a tiny bit more effort was required. "You will stay on the bench—and will not play in a game—until you have demonstrated to me in practice that you are ready to apply yourself with seriousness of purpose." He paused. "I am sorry, son."

Gary blinked in genuine surprise. He looked from Mr. Flynn to Mike Moseley. He would have wagered a week's allowance that Mike Moseley had argued for suspension—not just this time, but other times in the past. That was why he was here with Mr. Flynn. He had finally won his argument. Mike Moseley was always uptight.

7

Without another word, Mr. Flynn turned and walked away from Gary. Silently Mike Moseley followed him.

Outside in the corridor, Gary spotted Monica Conway, the coach of the Madison High girls' basketball team. She was waiting for Mike Moseley. Miss Conway and Coach Moseley were always together. They chaperoned most of the student dances and parties. Gary had seen them together at the movies. And the time he had taken Kimberly to dinner on her birthday, they were there—Miss Conway and Mike Moseley—seated at a table, having dinner together. That time, Gary had been surprised at the sight of Mike Moseley grinning and chattering just like anyone else. He never grinned and chattered on the basketball court.

Miss Conway smiled at Gary. "Hi," she said.

Gary grinned back at her. Monica Conway seemed nice, and she certainly didn't fit the stereotype of a female athletic coach. She was short and slender, almost delicately built. He had heard she was a dead-eye shot with a basketball, and a magician when it came to dribbling—a couple of skills that earned her a considerable measure of fame in college. She was pretty, with jet-black hair, cut short, and wraparound glasses that gave her face a sort of pixyish appearance. But most important, she was nice, always smiling and speaking to everyone. Gary had wondered more than once what she saw in the grouchy Mike Moseley. Maybe he was different around her, away from the school. Gary remembered the two of them laughing together at the restaurant table. But still,

Monica Conway dating Mike Moseley was, well, sort of like Kimberly Bennett dating Horse Mueller. They just didn't fit.

"Hi," Gary replied and walked on past her, heading for the staircase leading up to the gymnasium. Kimberly would be waiting for him. Howie Fenton and his girl friend, Barbara Sharpe, would be waiting with her. They were going to a party at Howie's house. The laughers and the gigglers would be there, not the frowners.

As he walked, Gary reflected for a moment on Mr. Flynn's pronouncement. Mr. Flynn had pulled one out of the hat this time. No warning at all—just whammo! The days of clowning around on Mr. Flynn's basketball team were at an end, for sure. Next time, probably, not just whammo, but double whammo! Out for good.

Gary did not relish the thought of keeping a stern countenance on the practice court—and for how long? Mr. Flynn did not say. Gary might practice and practice and practice and never get into a game again. He frowned. And even if he did get back into game action, he was to be just Gary Whipple, another substitute coming off the bench. No thrill in that.

At the foot of the stairs he turned and looked back down the corridor at Monica Conway and, as he skipped up the stairs, he grinned suddenly.

Chapter Two

"I want to come out for your basketball team," Gary said.

It was early on Monday afternoon, the last few minutes of the second lunch period at Madison High.

Gary was seated across the desk from Monica Conway in her small office alongside the dressing rooms. He had never been in her office before. The office looked like any other coach's office. There were calendar pages of the five months of the basketball season tacked to the wall. Practice sessions were marked in pencil. Game dates were noted in red lettering. There was a shelf containing books on basketball tactics and physical conditioning. There were two pictures on the wall. One was a framed photograph of a younger—not much younger, really—Monica Conway in a basketball uniform, poised for a shot at the basket. The other was a team picture—last season's Madison High Pirates, the girls' team she had coached to the quarterfinals of the state tournament.

Monica Conway sat behind an ancient wooden desk. She was wearing a bulky-knit turtleneck sweater, light brown with a white pattern on the front. With her youthful good looks and her large-lens wraparound glasses, she appeared poised for departure on a skiing trip, instead of being about to take the court for practice with a basketball team. She held a pencil in her hand, and for a moment she nibbled at the eraser, watching Gary.

Like everyone else in Madison by this time, Monica Conway knew that Mr. Flynn had benched Gary. She had probably been one of the first to learn the news. She would have heard from Mike Moseley, probably before they got out of the corridor and into the gymnasium on their way out of the building. But even without Mike Moseley, she could hardly have missed the wave of chatter sweeping the town over the weekend.

Gary had broken the news to his friends at the party at Howie's house on Friday night.

"You're kidding," Howie said. For once, Howie was frowning. "Did he really?"

"Yup."

"For how long?"

"I don't know."

"You don't know?"

"He didn't say, and I didn't ask."

"This is horrible," Kimberly said.

Gary grinned at her. He liked Kimberly. Nobody ever called her pretty, with her round face and turned-up nose. Her friends called her "cute." Gary liked her because she knew when to laugh. And now, because she knew when to pout.

"Well," Howie said slowly, still frowning, "it won't be forever."

11

Gary turned his grin to Howie. "You never know," he said.

Raymo leaned in. "You don't seem very worried about it."

"Are you up to something?" Howie asked.

Kimberly moved over in front of Gary and stared at his face. "You've got a funny look in your eye," she said.

"Which eye?" Gary asked, and everyone laughed, and the subject of Gary's suspension died away for the moment.

From the party at Howie's, and from whomever Mr. Flynn and Mike Moseley might have told, the word of Gary Whipple's benching spread rapidly.

Basketball news always traveled fast in Madison. The leading restaurant in town was called the Pirates' Den. Hamburgers were listed on the menu as pirate-burgers. In Madison during the late fall and winter months there were two major topics of conversation: the Pirates' last game and the Pirates' next game. So the word about Gary was everywhere.

Nobody was alarmed about the temporary loss of Gary Whipple's basketball talents. A close student of the game might be concerned about the loss of bench strength. Successful basketball teams need good play-ers in the sixth and seventh positions. They provide valuable minutes of rest for the starters. They move in to fill the void when a starter gets himself in foul trouble. But nobody thought Gary Whipple was a crucial cog in the mighty basketball machine of Mad-ison High. He was valuable as a substitute, but not vital to victory.

However, there was something to mourn. Victories

and losses were not involved. The Madison High Pirates were sure to roll on, powerful as ever. But who was going to dribble on his knees now? Who was going to startle an opposing guard out of his wits by faking a throw in the face? Who would take a bow to acknowledge the cheers for a field goal?

The coffee drinkers in the Pirates' Den on Saturday morning bemoaned the loss of Gary Whipple. The men getting their hair cut in John's barber shop on Saturday afternoon expressed the hope that Orville Flynn would not keep Gary on the bench for long. The people eating dinner in the Pirates' Den on Saturday night discussed the loss with people at the next table. And the people coming out of church on Sunday morning talked about it on the sidewalk.

As for Gary, he spent the weekend shrugging and smiling. Some offered the opinion that he was taking it well. Others, knowing Gary and noticing the look in his eye, wondered if he were not more amused than distressed by the turn of events. After all, he was again center stage.

At home, Gary's father sighed and spoke past him in mock rebuke: "Mother, if this boy had had a few brothers and sisters, we would not be having these problems."

Gary had heard the line before, implying that an only child grew up used to having all eyes on him alone. Gary gave his standard response: "How about you? You came from a family of five." His father's three brothers and sister regaled family gatherings with recollections of his father's boyhood antics. Gary knew about his father.

His father smiled at him briefly. Then, in a serious

13

tone, he asked, "What now, funnyman? Are you going to straighten up your act and play basketball, or are you going to just call it quits?"

"I think I'm going to play basketball," Gary said.

Something in Gary's tone caused his father to lift an eyebrow. But he said nothing.

Gary's mother looked at him. "You've got a funny look in your eye," she said.

"Huh?"

"That look in your eye," she said slowly.

"Oh," Gary said. He paused. "That's what Kimberly said."

Through all the chatter and conversation and commentary of the weekend in Madison, there was not a single word of criticism of Orville Flynn. Even Kimberly's "This is horrible" suggested no blame of Orville Flynn. Throughout the town, nobody questioned the coach's action. After all, Orville Flynn had brought home three state championship trophies to Madison. His teams had been runner-up to the champion in two other years. Orville Flynn's Madison High Pirates were always up there with the winners. As sad and lamentable as the incident might be, Orville Flynn had made the right decision. Orville Flynn always made the right decision. Of that, everyone in Madison was certain.

At school on Monday morning, Gary had moved through his classes acknowledging the condolences from students and teachers alike: "Tough luck," "Too bad," and, "It won't last forever."

To all of them, Gary grinned and shrugged.

Once, in midmorning, Gary encountered Monica

Conway. She was coming up a staircase. Gary was going down the stairs. With a left turn at the bottom, the corridor led toward Gary's next class.

"I heard the bad news," she said. "I'm awfully sorry. But don't worry. It will work itself out."

Gary smiled at her. "Yes, I'm sure it will," he said.

Perhaps it was the way he said it. Perhaps it was the look in his eye as he smiled at her. Whatever it was, Monica Conway was still standing there looking down at him when Gary turned the corner at the bottom of the staircase and glanced up.

Ever since Monica Conway had come to Madison High two years ago, Gary had considered her to be cool, neat, friendly—all the good words. But until now, seated across the desk from her in her office, he never realized how cool Monica Conway really was.

He had finished the brief, simple statement of his intentions. Now he waited. Her expression did not change. She was looking him in the eye.

She had to say something—yes, no, maybe. She had to accept, reject, laugh, shout, panic, faint—something. Why didn't she? But she just sat there, looking at him. Gary came to the conclusion she was not surprised. Neither was she alarmed. A bit nervously, Gary grinned at her.

"I suppose that I must ask this question," she said finally, "although I think I already know the answer: Why do you want to play on the girls' team?"

Gary, his grin gone, returned her gaze. "Mr. Flynn has benched me. He won't let me play in any games with his team. So I want to play on your team."

15

She watched Gary in silence for a moment. Then, softly, she said, "Ummmm." She laid the pencil on the desk and, speaking evenly, she said, "And you don't think I'd jerk you out of a game and park you on the bench for clowning just as quickly as Mr. Flynn did."

She spoke the words as a statement of fact, but she was asking a question. Gary had his answer ready. "Yes, but I won't clown."

She seemed to accept his promise without blinking and took the conversation back to her original question. "But getting benched by Mr. Flynn, that's not the complete answer, is it? I mean, that's not the real reason you want to play for the girls' team, is it?" She was looking at him in a funny way.

Gary knew what she was asking. Sure, he could promise not to clown, and he could keep the promise. Why clown? Just playing on the team—a boy, a member of the girls' team—would have to be the best caper in the history of Madison High. For good, crazy fun, it beat dribbling on the knees any night of the week.

But all Gary said was, "Huh?"

"Never mind," she said. She picked up the pencil again and stared at it for a moment. A slight frown creased her forehead. She seemed to be weighing her thoughts carefully. Then she looked up and said, "You know that I coach a team of girls. We play our games against teams of girls. Mr. Flynn coaches a team of boys, and they play against teams of boys. You are a boy. That is where you belong, on the boys' team. Don't you agree?"

"But, Mr. Flynn—"

"I know."

"Well, I . . ."

Monica Conway leaned back in the chair and waited while Gary searched for the words he wanted. She seemed to know what he was going to say next.

"If I can't play on the boys' team, why can't I play on the girls' team? It works the other way—girls on boys' teams—in basketball, soccer, baseball, even football. I've read about it."

"Yes, yes, I know," she said. "But it's not really all that simple. What if other boys decide to follow your example? What happens to the boys' team then? What happens to the girls' team? Or look at it the other way. What if one of my girls decides she wants to try out for the boys' team?" She paused. "You can see where it all could lead."

The thought had never entered Gary's mind. He considered Monica Conway's words for a moment. Then he shrugged his shoulders and discarded the idea. There was not a single player on Mr. Flynn's team—not even Howie, who enjoyed a gag almost as much as Gary—who would consider the move for a moment. As for a girl going out for the boys' team— well, it was simply ridiculous. No girl could play for the Pirates boys' team. She would sit on the bench with the substitutes. So why would a girl even want to try? No, Monica Conway's warning was not dangerous at all.

"I don't think. . . ."

"Well, perhaps." Monica smiled at him.

Monica leaned forward in her chair. "Gary, this

may come as a surprise to you—I'm sure it will—but it will explain what we've been talking about." She paused. "I am one of the small minority who believe that we should have one varsity team, composed of both boys and girls."

Gary blinked at her. "Really?" he said.

"Really. I don't believe in second-class citizenship for girls. If a girl is good enough to play on the varsity, she should be allowed to play on the varsity. She should not be relegated to some sort of second team confined to girls only."

Gary stared at her. Then he said, "You mean that I can?"

Monica Conway shrugged her shoulders and leaned back. "As far as I'm concerned," she said.

But of course Monica Conway was not the only one concerned.

Gary had barely settled into his seat in Mrs. Miller's American history class when the door opened. A student clerk entered and handed Mrs. Miller a slip of paper. Mrs. Miller read the note, glanced at Gary, and then motioned Gary to come to her desk. He was wanted in the principal's office.

Gary followed the girl out of the classroom and down the corridor toward the office.

"Here it goes," he told himself with a grin.

In the principal's office, George Gordon, balding, heavyset, reddish faced, seeming perpetually out of breath, was seated at his desk. Monica Conway was in an overstuffed chair to the left of Mr. Gordon's desk. Orville Flynn was on a sofa to the right.

18

From the outer office, the student clerks and the people on the administrative staff were peering at the developing scene. Gary Whipple was no stranger to Mr. Gordon's office. His pranks landed him there with regularity. Neither were the coaches strangers to Mr. Gordon's office. They had the business of their teams to discuss with the principal. But all three at the same time?

Taking a deep breath, Mr. Gordon got to his feet, walked to the door, closed it, and returned to his desk.

"Sit down, Gary," he said.

Gary took a seat on the sofa next to Orville Flynn.

Mr. Gordon settled himself in the chair behind his desk. He laid his hands, fingers spread, flat on the desktop. He looked at Gary for a moment without speaking. Then, with an air of resignation, he said, "Gary, you can do this, if you really want to."

Gary nodded and waited.

"Title IX of the Federal Aid to Education Act prohibits discrimination on the basis of sex," Mr. Gordon said. "Trouble is, it does not define discrimination. Does the law mean that anyone—male or female—has the right to play on any team? Or does it mean that a school is required to offer equal facilities—a girls' team for every boys' team, and vice versa—in every sport?" He took a deep breath and sighed. "Nobody knows."

Mr. Gordon leaned back and frowned, clearly a man unhappy with the facts he was being forced to recite.

"Some school districts have barred mixed competi-

19

tion. Ours has no rule on the subject. Some conferences have rules against mixed competition. The Black Hawk Big Seven Conference doesn't. Some state high school associations prohibit boys and girls from competing against each other in certain sports. In Illinois, the only rule applies to state tournaments."

Gary could imagine the frantic flurry of telephone calls touched off by Monica Conway's announcement of Gary's request. First, the school district office. Then, the Black Hawk Big Seven Conference headquarters. And finally, with fading hope, the state high school athletic association office in Bloomington. He could picture the faces involved—Mr. Gordon, getting redder and more breathless; Orville Flynn, unchanging, hiding whatever thoughts he had behind a calm exterior; and Monica Conway, interested, attentive, and probably already knowing the answers Mr. Gordon was seeking.

"So, as I told you, you can do this if you really want to," Mr. Gordon said. "The question now is: Do you really want to do this?" He paused. "Or is this just another . . ." He let his questioning expression finish the sentence for him.

"Yes, sir."

"Yes what?"

"Yes, sir. I want to do this."

Mr. Gordon stared at Gary for a moment. Then he cast a glance, not a friendly one, at Monica Conway. She sat quite still, expressionless.

"All right," Mr. Gordon said softly, with an air of resignation.

The meeting was over. Gary stood. He nodded slightly. He walked to the door. He opened it and walked out. He grinned at the gawkers in the outer office. He stepped into the corridor and turned toward his classroom.

Alone in the corridor, he stretched his arms high over his head and grinned broadly.

"I'm making history," he said aloud, "and there's nothing to it. Nothing to it."

Or so he thought.

Chapter Three

"You're wacko," Howie Fenton told him. Howie was not laughing. He was not even smiling. "Completely wacko."

Gary was dressing for practice in the boys' locker room. All around him the boys were coming out of the showers and climbing into their street clothes. For them, practice was over. They had vacated the basketball court. It was time for the girls' team to take over. Gary was stripping off his street clothes and getting into his uniform.

"That is precisely the right word—wacko," said Horse Mueller, walking past them. As always, Horse looked as though he had just received some really bad news and at the same time was detecting an unpleasant odor. He wore a towel around his waist and kept walking, without waiting for a reply from Gary.

"Do you know what you're doing?" Howie asked, leaning in close.

"Sure," Gary said. "I'm changing teams. But don't worry, we won't be playing against each other. It's not as if I'm going over to the enemy."

"Holy cow!"

Gary held up his uniform shirt, bright green with a

golden "11" on the front and back. He turned the shirt slowly. "I wonder if they'll have to give me a new number," he said absently. "Somebody may already be wearing number 11."

Raymo Bailey, Howie's partner at starting forward, came out of the shower and stopped in front of Gary, staring. "Is this all true? Is this really happening?"

Across the room, Gary saw Mike Moseley staring at him. Gary grinned at Moseley. Moseley frowned.

Gary turned back to Raymo. "Please, please, not all these questions before practice," he said with mock exasperation. "I must concentrate. I owe it to my teammates."

"Holy cow!" Howie said again, and he turned and headed for the showers.

Gary pulled on the shirt and walked out of the dressing room, heading for the stairs leading to the basketball court.

On the court, he was alone. He walked to the edge of the court and picked up a ball. Absently, he dribbled a couple of times and shot toward the basket. He missed. Running forward, he picked off the rebound and dribbled back out toward the edge of the keyhole. He turned and shot again. He missed again.

The girls began coming through the door and onto the court.

First was Frances Holcott. Frances was the starting center, a tall girl—within an inch of Gary's height—with short-cropped reddish hair and a face full of freckles. Gary knew Frances. He had two classes with her. He liked her. She was friendly. She always smiled at him when he called her Red. Somehow, Frances looked larger now, taller, sturdier in her basketball uniform than she seemed in the jeans and shirts she wore to class.

"Hi ya, Red," Gary called out.

"Hi, Gary." Frances gave him a little smile.

By the time the second face, that of Rita Cranston, appeared through the doorway, it was obvious to Gary that Monica Conway had delivered an announcement to her assembled players before sending them out onto the court.

Frances had not appeared surprised by the sight of Gary on the court.

Neither was Rita surprised. She gave Gary a brief glance and a nod and headed for a loose ball at the edge of the court. She picked it up and dribbled toward the basket. She laid the ball up easily. It rolled around the rim and dropped through.

Same ol' man-hater Rita, Gary thought. Rita was a junior, a year younger than Gary. But he knew her. Howie had dated her during the summer. What a dud at a party she was, always serious, scowling, talking about heavy things. She was a feminist, always complaining that it was a man's world. Howie got his fill the night she called him a male chauvinist pig. Rita ought to be dating Horse Mueller. They could be unhappy together. She was short, probably no more than five feet three inches tall, and she played guard. Gary had heard she was good—quick, a sure-handed dribbler and passer, and an accurate shooter from the outside.

Gary shrugged and turned away from her.

Pamela Hunt came bubbling through the door. Pamela was Kimberly's best friend. She had wide eyes, blue as a summer sky, and yellow hair, long and flowing, which she wore tied at the back of her neck for basketball. She was smiling. Pamela was always smiling.

"Hi, teammate," Gary said.

"Kimberly is going to kill you," she said.

"Me?"

"You."

"She can't kill me. She's a cheerleader and I'm a player. Cheerleaders can't kill players."

Pamela wrinkled her nose at Gary and moved on toward the end of the court where Frances and Rita were taking shots. Pamela was not one of the best basketball players. Gary remembered her complaints about not getting much playing time. But she was a ray of bright sunshine after the icy greeting from Rita Cranston.

The other girls trailed out the door and onto the court. Gary knew them all, at least by sight. There was Debbie Robinson, Rita's partner at guard. She was followed by Ruth Kovacs. Gary had a history class with Ruth. Then came Sharon Richardson, Sandy Young—all of them. They met Gary's happy greetings with grins or glares or the kind of curiosity one shows about a new animal at the zoo.

Monica Conway, wearing slacks and a sweatshirt, with a whistle dangling on a chain around her neck, was last out the door.

By that time, the players were a crowd at the end of the court, keeping a half-dozen balls in the air, peppering the backboard, the rim, the net.

Gary barely noticed Monica Conway's arrival and did not notice at all the group of boys halfway up in the bleacher seats until someone shouted: "Hey, Gary, you're lookin' mighty sweet out there."

Gary turned in the direction of the shout. Howie and Raymo and Hubie Thompson were sitting in a row. Gary grinned and waved.

Monica Conway, striding past Gary, was not smiling. "Go ahead with your warm-up," she said as she walked. Her voice was brisk and businesslike, with none of the friendly softness Gary had always heard when he met her in the corridor.

She marched to the side of the court, toward the boys.

Behind her, everybody had stopped shooting. Nobody was moving. The court was quiet. They were all watching.

Monica turned back to the players on the court. "I said, go ahead with your warm-ups," she announced.

The players, Gary included, began to dribble and shoot for the basket.

Out of the corner of his eye, Gary saw her standing there, below the boys, with the boys all staring down at her. She was saying something. They were listening. Gary could not hear her words. Then she turned her attention back to her players on the court. Behind her, the boys slowly left the bleacher seats and walked out the door at the end of the gymnasium.

Only when she brought the squad together at the center of the court did Gary, looking at the faces around him, come to the sudden realization: He did not know this basketball team.

The players on the boys' team, for the most part, had been his teammates and opponents for years, since grade school. He knew their strengths and their weaknesses. He knew their limits. He knew their inclinations. And they knew these things about him, too.

But this basketball team was different. He had never practiced with the players. He had never even seen them practice. He never had played in a game with a single one of them. And when it came to seeing them play a game, he could claim no more than a passing glance. Normally, the girls' games and the boys' games made up a doubleheader. The girls played first, the boys second. Sometimes Gary was in the bleachers during the first half of a girls' game, before heading to the dressing room. But he never was a very attentive spectator. There was always something more fun for Gary Whipple than watching another team—especially a girls' team—play basketball.

As people, the girls were not strangers to him—not Frances, not Rita, not Pamela, not any of them—but as basketball players they were total strangers.

The realization bothered Gary.

"Coach, I—"

Monica turned to Gary when he spoke. "Gary, my players call me Monica," she said.

"Okay."

"What is it? You started to say something."

Gary changed his mind. He decided to keep his ignorance to himself—his ignorance of his new teammates, his ignorance of the style of play.

"Nothing," he said finally.

He decided that his ignorance did not matter because a boy among girls on a basketball court was not going to have any problems.

The scrimmage was five minutes old. They were five to a side, Gary and four girls versus five girls. Monica was both the coach and the referee. She raced up and down the court with the action, calling the fouls and whistling the play to a halt to make substitutions.

At first, it had been fun.

"Is it a foul if I guard too close?" Gary piped with a silly leer on his face.

Pamela Hunt giggled and grinned at Gary. She had the bluest eyes. Frances Holcott showed a small smile. Frances always was friendly. Rita Cranston wore an expression of disgust. Rita still reminded Gary of Horse Mueller. Monica Conway wore no expression at all. She stared at Gary through the large-lens wraparound glasses. She said nothing.

Finally Gary looked away, shrugged, and took up his position with the Green team, opposing the Gold team.

Now, with the score 8-6 in favor of the Gold team, Gary played with a deepening frown on his face.

His Green team was trailing. That was bad. But he had scored two of his team's field goals. That was good. But still. . .

Something was gnawing at Gary. He could not identify it. In the racing around the court—the fierce defense work, the intense dribbling, the passing, the rebounding—the uneasy feeling remained there, stuck in his mind. Something was wrong. Something was amiss. Something was not working.

But what?

Gary took in a pass from Debbie Robinson. He turned and dribbled twice. He was just over the center stripe. He made his way toward the edge of the keyhole. He turned to pass off to Sharon Richardson to his right.

And then—he did not have the ball.

He had thought he was passing. He had felt the ball leave his fingers. But then he knew he had not passed the ball. The ball simply had left his fingers.

He heard the *thump-thump* of a dribble and turned.

To his left, Rita Cranston, bent low, was dribbling the other way, across the center stripe. She stopped, looked, and fired a pass to Ruth Kovacs. Ruth drove under the basket and laid the ball up for a field goal.

Gary, empty-handed and gaping at mid-court, suddenly was able to identify the thought that had been gnawing at his mind since the start of the scrimmage. Some of these girls were pretty good basketball players.

He wanted to dig his way through the floor and hide. But that was impossible. He dreaded looking around. Rita was sure to give him a sneer of triumph. Frances might be smiling. Pamela, always quick with a giggle, would more likely give her friend a look of sympathy, which would be worse than a giggle. Gary could imagine Monica Conway's questioning glance.

Finally he looked around. The members of his Green team were bringing the ball back into play.

Rita was guarding the dribbler, too busy to give Gary a triumphant sneer. Nobody was looking at Gary. Everyone was moving.

Gary rushed to join the action.

Then, barely minutes later, with his Green team driving toward the basket, Gary worked himself free just inside the free-throw line. He took in a pass from Debbie. He whirled. He shot. The shot, a soft floater of the kind that usually finds its way into the nets, hit the back of the rim. The ball bounced up. Coming down, it nicked the side of the rim and bounced away.

Gary, moving in as a follow-up to his shot, went for the rebound. He leaped. He reached out. He was right on target. He felt the ball on his fingertips.

And then—*whack!*

His leap came to an end. The ball left his outstretched fingers. The floor, shiny with varnish, came into view. The floor came up to him. The floor hit him. He felt pain—his hip, the side of a knee, the palm of one hand, the other elbow.

He rolled over.

Frances was bending over him. She extended a hand.

"I'm sorry," she said.

Gary took her hand. He got to his feet. He managed a half-smile.

The gnawing thought certainly was no mystery now.

Showering after practice, Gary had the boys' dressing room to himself. The room was silent except for

30

the gushing sound of water rushing out of the shower-head. Gary had never experienced such absolute silence in a dressing room. It was spooky.

Finally he was able to check his wounds. There had been no opportunity at the moment of the spill, with Frances standing there apologizing and Rita and all the others standing around staring at him.

He twisted around and stared at his hip. No question, he was going to wind up with a dandy bruise. Nothing serious, but still a dandy bruise. It would not show. His elbow and the side of his knee and the palm of his hand bore the badges of an aggressive basketball player—floor burns. The hot water of the shower stung the floor burns. Gary shrugged off the stinging sensation. It was nothing new. He had had bruises and floor burns before.

"But never delivered by a girl," he mumbled to himself.

Toweling off, Gary forgot the ache in his hip and the stinging of the floor burns. Two other thoughts were pressing in on his mind: Rita *is* quick. And: Frances *is* strong.

Gary frowned as he stuffed in his shirt, buckled his trousers, and bent over to tie his shoes.

"They don't play much like girls," he said aloud to the empty dressing room. He remembered his rare glimpses of the girls in gym class playing basketball. They fumbled. They stumbled. They flailed their arms. They shut their eyes in close contact. They panted helplessly and begged for a rest period. That was the way girls played basketball. "They don't play much like girls," Gary repeated.

He pulled on his jacket, scooped his books out of the bottom of the locker, and walked out of the dressing room.

Monica was waiting in the corridor.

"Are you all right?" she asked.

"Who, me?"

"That was a nasty spill."

"Ah, it was nothing."

"Are you sure?"

"Sure."

"See you tomorrow." Monica turned and walked back toward the girls' dressing room.

"Yeah," Gary said, and headed up the stairs for the walk home. He wished she had not asked about his bruises and scrapes.

Chapter Four

Walking home, Gary succeeded in shoving to the back of his mind the memory of Rita Cranston stealing the ball out of his hands and the memory of Frances Holcott knocking him flying.

Well, almost to the back of his mind.

As he walked the eight blocks home in the fading sunlight of the late afternoon, the twin spectres kept reappearing before his eyes. The twin spectres were not pleasant.

He touched the bruised hip. He felt a twinge of pain. He remembered Monica Conway's expression of concern: "That was a nasty spill."

"Humph," Gary said aloud to the empty street. He was not about to tell the coach—a woman coach, above all, even if she was Monica Conway—about the pain. He was not about to admit that a girl—a girl, above all—had caused him any problems on the basketball court.

For a moment Gary relived the impact of the collision. Being walloped from the blind side while in the air was no fun. The unexpected jolt reverberated from his scalp to the soles of his feet. And the floor was a mighty hard landing place for a hip, an elbow, a knee, a hand. Even worse than the pain in some ways was being the loser in a collision. Losing was damaging to the ego. And Frances Holcott was a girl!

He recalled the empty—the really empty—feeling of finding himself without the ball when Rita plucked it from his hands. He remembered the picture of Rita dribbling away from him. Losing the ball to a steal anytime had to be one of the worst feelings in basketball. One moment you had the ball. The next, you didn't. Suddenly you were standing there with your hands extended, holding nothing but air. It was embarrassing. And Rita Cranston was a girl!

But more than the memory of the events on the practice court was haunting Gary's mind as he walked along.

If the Pirates had a girl like Rita Cranston, who could steal the ball from him, and if they had a girl like Frances Holcott, who could send him crashing to the floor, then maybe the other teams, the opponents, had them, too. Not just maybe. Probably.

Maybe not as quick as Rita. But maybe quick enough. Perhaps not as strong as Frances. But strong enough. Maybe. Perhaps. Probably.

The thought had first flickered through Gary's mind when Rita stole the ball out of his hands. It was a fleeting thought, barely recognized, and then lost in the heat of the play that followed. The thought returned, a little stronger, when he crashed to the floor after colliding with Frances. And now, walking alone in the late-afternoon dusk, the thought was there again—this time more clearly defined, disconcerting, inescapable.

At the time of the steal Gary had been grateful that

Monica Conway had sent Howie and Raymo and Hubie out of the gymnasium and away from the practice. They would have howled at the sight of him standing there, arms outstretched, hands empty, the ball gone. He had been glad, too, that they were not there to see Frances send him sprawling. He would have heard about that one for weeks.

Sure, the word was bound to get around—both Rita's steal and Frances' jolting blow. The girls would talk, same as the boys would talk. But his friends— Howie, Raymo, Hubie—would not be able to give eyewitness accounts. They had not seen it happen. They might ask. But they had not been there to see it, and that was good.

A game would be different, however. Monica Conway could not send the onlookers away. She could not clear the gymnasium of spectators. They would be there. Howie and Raymo and Hubie would be there. Mr. Flynn would be watching. So would Mike Moseley. Kimberly would be on the sideline with the cheerleaders, watching. His parents would be in the seats. So would about two thousand other people.

Gary shuddered. The crowd was supposed to be an important part of the whole gag. The caper, to be any fun at all, needed the laughs of the crowd. But what if. . .

Gary tried to recall the girls' basketball games he had seen. He tried to remember the opponents. Did they have the likes of Rita Cranston, flitting around the court stealing the ball? Did they have their own Frances Holcott, a menace to health, safety, and ego, operating under the backboards? He couldn't remember.

35

Monica Conway had coached the Pirates to the quarterfinals of the girls' state tournament. So the Pirates must have been pretty good, among the best teams in the state. Maybe the reason for their success was that they had their Rita Cranston and their Frances Holcott, and the other teams did not.

Gary concluded that *was* the reason and took some comfort in the conclusion.

He turned the last corner and cut across the yard, heading for the wide porch across the front of his house. He took a deep breath and managed a smile to himself. He would shove the troublesome moments of his first practice with the girls' team to the back of his mind. Everything was going to work out. He skipped up the four steps and crossed the porch, opened the front door, and walked in.

His father, watching the evening news on television, glanced up, peered at Gary over his glasses, and slowly shook his head from side to side.

"You've heard," Gary said, with a wide grin. He was surprised at the effort required to produce the wide grin. Suddenly, for no reason at all, he had a mental picture of Rita stealing the ball out of his hands in front of two thousand laughing fans. Next, like the evening news on the television screen, there was a picture of Frances knocking him into a cartwheel while the crowd cheered. And through it all, his father was shaking his head slowly from side to side.

"I've heard," his father said.

Gary's mother came in from the kitchen. "Your father has had a difficult afternoon," she said.

36

"Oh?"

"Well," his father said, "what does a man say when people ask about his son going out for the girls' basketball team?"

Gary laughed. "Yeah, it's funny, isn't it?"

"Yes, funny," his father said. But he was not laughing.

Gary's mother turned and went back to the kitchen. At the same time his father got up, walked across to the television set, and turned it off. Gary watched his mother leave. He watched his father cross the room and click off the television set. The movements of the two, seeming almost choreographed, made Gary lift his eyebrows.

"Uh-oh," Gary said aloud.

"Yes, uh-oh," his father said, returning to his chair. "Have a seat." He waved at the sofa. "We're going to have a little talk."

Gary parked himself on the edge of the sofa. "Are you going to try to talk me out of it?"

"No."

"Well, then. . ."

"Mr. Gordon is quite worried about what effect this might have on the girls' basketball program, even what effect it might have on the boys' program— where it all might lead."

"He called you?"

"Yes. He's quite concerned."

"What's it going to hurt?"

"Monica Conway explained to you what this could lead to, didn't she?"

"Nobody is going to quit the boys' team for the

37

girls' team—not Howie, not anybody. And none of the girls are going to switch to the boys' team. Why would they?"

"Why did you?"

"Aw, c'mon."

"Do you think you hold the exclusive franchise for silly ideas?"

Gary grinned slightly. "It sounds to me like a lot of fun," he said. "And it's not going to hurt anybody."

"Some people think it could cause a lot of trouble."

"Monica Conway doesn't. I think she sort of liked the idea."

"Don't make the mistake of misunderstanding Monica Conway. Mr. Gordon explained her position to me. Because of her own personal feelings—her principles—she felt she couldn't say no to you. But remember, she did not recruit you for this. It wasn't her idea. She did not encourage you. And I would not be surprised to find out she doesn't want you. Her strong principles left her no choice but to accept you. But perhaps even Monica Conway, with her unusual ideas on the subject, is wondering if this is the right time and the right place, and, yes, if you are the right person for this sort of thing."

"Have you talked with her?"

"No."

"Well, she didn't say anything like that when I talked to her in her office." Gary paused. "And Mr. Gordon didn't even ask me to change my mind."

Gary's father sighed. "No, I know. He simply explained the situation."

Gary nodded. His father had said he was not trying

to change his mind. But he was pushing for a recon-
sideration. The message was clear, and Gary was
troubled by it. His father never had applauded his
antics. But at the same time he had never laid down
any ultimatums, demanding that Gary cut out the
joking. This was not an ultimatum, either, but it was
closer to one than anything Gary could recall.

"Did Mr. Gordon ask you to tell me not to do it?"

"No."

"Did he ask you to try to talk me out of it."

"No. He just expressed his concern and asked that I
talk with you about it."

"Uh-huh."

"Gary, there always comes a time when there are
other things more important than a laugh. You'll have
to learn that."

Gary started to say again, "It'll be a lot of fun and
it won't hurt anybody." But instead he said simply,
"Okay."

The conversation was over. Gary picked up his
school books from the sofa and walked into his room.
He tossed the books on the bed. He wondered why his
father, a certified jokester when he was a boy, didn't
like the idea of the best caper in the world. This one
was going to be great. And, he repeated to himself,
who's to get hurt? Oh, well.

His mother's head in the doorway interrupted his
thoughts.

"Call Kimberly," she said. "She's called twice. And
make it quick. Dinner is almost ready."

"Okay."

Gary walked into the hallway and turned into the

little alcove where the telephone rested on a tiny desk. He dropped into the chair and dialed Kimberly's number. The phone barely completed the first ring. Kimberly answered.

"Hi," Gary said.

"This is terrible," she blurted.

"Terrible? It's wonderful."

"Wonderful? It's terrible."

Gary grinned. "Am I talking to myself?" he asked.

"You're going to be talking to yourself, Mr. Gary Whipple."

There was a moment of silence. Then Kimberly said, "Barbara called me. Howie told her. She could hardly talk for laughing."

Gary's grin widened. This was fun. The horrible moment when Rita stole the ball out of his hands was far back in his mind. The painful memory of Frances' crashing blow was fading away. Even the somber words of his father grew dim.

"I'm making history," Gary said. "They laughed at Christopher Columbus when he said the world was round. They scoffed at Marco Polo when he headed for China. They made fun of Henry Ford's horseless carriage. They—"

"My boyfriend . . . on the girls' basketball team!"

"Be proud," Gary proclaimed.

"What am I going to do?"

"Do? Cheer for me, that's what."

"Cheer for you!"

"Sure. You're a cheerleader, aren't you?"

"Good grief!"

The line was silent a moment and then—click!

Gary stared at the telephone. Then he replaced it in its cradle. Kimberly really didn't like the idea. Kimberly, of all people. Gary scratched his head. It was the caper of the century. Sure, Horse Mueller frowned. He always frowned. Sure, Mike Moseley was angry about the idea. Mike Moseley seemed angry about everything Gary did. Sure, Mr. Gordon was upset. He always got upset. But Howie—Howie was frowning instead of laughing. And his father's serious talk was something new.

Now Kimberly. Kimberly always loved a gag as much as Gary. Maybe she didn't like hearing it first from Barbara. Maybe that was the problem. Well, Gary had had no chance to tell her during the afternoon. Maybe she objected to his spending all that time—practicing, playing in games, riding the team van—with a crowd of girls. But how could anyone be jealous of Rita Cranston?

"Who knows?" Gary mumbled to himself. "A caper sure can get complicated sometimes."

Chapter Five

Never before had such a crowd swamped the old yellow-brick gymnasium at Madison High at such an early hour on game night.

As usual, it was a doubleheader: the Madison High Pirates versus the Bennington High Falcons, with the girls' game starting at seven o'clock and the boys' game at eight-fifteen.

The crowd always was sparse for the tip-off of the girls' game. The bleachers were dotted with parents, girl friends of the players, boyfriends of the players, and practically no one else. The main body of the crowd normally started streaming through the front doors and into the bleacher seats around the half time of the girls' game. The boys' team—"our Pirates"— was the team that the Madison High fans turned out in large numbers to cheer.

But here it was just a few minutes before six-thirty when Gary arrived, and already the street in front of the gymnasium was filled with people shuffling their way to the door. Inside, the lobby was a mass of milling people.

Somebody shouted, "Hey, Gary!"

Somebody else called out, "There he is!"

Gary grinned and waved a hand as he skipped up

the steps. He moved across the porch and stepped into the lobby. He weaved his way through the crowd and stepped through the door to the edge of the basketball court. Somebody in the bleachers called his name, and he waved a hand as he circled the court, heading for the stairs leading to the dressing rooms below.

Downstairs, in the empty corridor leading to the boys' dressing room, Gary's smile faded. He felt a touch of nervousness. He felt the same way he had that night last season, in the first game of the district tournament, when he knew he was going to start in place of Raymo Bailey, who was sidelined with the flu. That time he had been nervous, noticeably so, in front of all his teammates in the locker room. This time he was alone with his nervousness. This was better.

Why nervous? Gary knew why.

Sure, the day at school, and then hanging around downtown in the afternoon at the drugstore, the record shop, the Pirates' Den had been fun. There had been a lot of laughs.

"Don't blame you a bit, Gary ol' boy," somebody had sung out in the corridor between classes. "Pamela Hunt is better looking than anyone on the boys' team."

Gary had laughed. Everybody had laughed—everybody, that is, except Kimberly, walking at Gary's side. Kimberly had frowned.

And then somebody had called out to Kimberly, "Watch out that you don't become the first cheerleader ever to lose her boyfriend to one of his teammates."

Everybody thought it was funny—everybody, that is, except Kimberly.

With all the wisecracks and laughter, Gary began to understand why Kimberly, who always loved his gags, hadn't like this one from the start.

Gary grinned at one of Kimberly's frowns and said, "It's Rita Cranston you've got to worry about. She's got the warmest smile, and she's crazy about me."

Kimberly's frown stayed in place.

"Ouch," Gary said.

But Kimberly aside, the world was laughing with Gary, even in the classroom. Old Mr. Benson, standing at the head of his English class, shoved his glasses back up the ridge of his nose with a long forefinger and offered his comment: "We've all heard of transfer students, of course, but this one takes the cake." The class howled.

Even at home, at the dinner table, Gary's parents managed to take a lighter view than Gary had expected. "You're going ahead with this," his father said. It was not a question but a statement of fact.

Their eyes met. To Gary, his father seemed to be saying, "I relayed Mr. Gordon's concerns. From there, the decision was yours." They both, it seemed to Gary, were thinking the same thing: his father had enjoyed a good gag as a boy.

Gary nodded in acknowledgment of his father's statement. "Are you going to be there for the historic event?" he asked.

"Do I have to?"

"Sure."

"Okay," his father said, "but I may disguise myself with a fake beard."

Gary grinned.

But now, walking to his locker in the deathly quiet of the boys' dressing room, the laughter seemed far behind Gary, and the feeling of queasy nervousness stayed with him.

Gary quickly peeled off his street clothes, put on his green game uniform, trimmed in gold, and walked out into the corridor and down toward the girls' dressing room. For a moment he was tempted to shout, "Here I come, ready or not." The cry was sure to set off a round of squeals. But he said nothing. Then he heard Monica's voice: "Is Whipple out there in the corridor?"

A head was poked out the door. It was Ruth Kovacs. She shouted back into the dressing room. "Yeah, he's here." She grinned at Gary. "Hi, Gary."

"Hi, teammate."

Again, Gary heard Monica's voice. "All right, girls, let's go."

The girls began filing out of the dressing room past Gary—Ruth Kovacs, Rita Cranston, Pamela Hunt, and then Monica Conway.

The coach fell into step beside Gary. "I don't know who's going to say what up there," she said, "but I am sure of what you are going to say."

Gary glanced at her, puzzled. Then he said, "Oh, like nothing, you mean."

"Exactly," she said. "Like nothing."

"What . . . is . . . that?"

The words came as individual shouts, each separated from the other by a long pause.

The Pirates, first on the court, were a couple of

minutes into their warm-up shots when the Bennington Falcons walked through the door to take the court. Gary had seen the blur of the blue uniforms out of the corner of his eye. He had fought down the impulse to turn and stare. He wondered if they had their own Rita Cranston. But instead of staring, he raced under the basket and picked off a rebound.

But now he heard shouted *"What . . . is . . . that?"* He turned. He looked up to see a woman, lanky, with short-cropped blond hair, wearing slacks and a blue sweatshirt with *Falcons* printed in silver on the front. Beyond her, a group of girls in blue uniforms with silver trim stood motionless. They were looking at him. Gary had never seen the woman before. She was pointing a finger at him. But she was not looking at Gary. She was pointing her face the other way, toward Monica, who was now walking across the court to meet the woman.

"Is . . . that . . . a . . . boy?"

The shouted words, again punctuated with pauses, ricocheted off the walls of the gymnasium, now quiet after the first shouted question.

"I think she might be talking about me," Gary said in a stage whisper.

Rita scowled at Gary. Frances rolled her eyes. Pamela giggled.

"Liz," Monica said calmly. "I tried to call you. I left a message for you. Didn't you get my message?"

"Message? What message?"

That was the last that Gary heard. Monica gently turned the woman named Liz away from the court. One by one, the Pirates resumed their warm-ups, taking a shot at the basket or dribbling in for a lay-up.

46

The Bennington players, after a confused moment of staring, first at Gary and then at the two coaches, moved to the other end of the court and began their warm-ups.

Ten minutes later, at the sideline, the players gathered around Monica for the final moments before the start of the game. She answered their questioning gazes. "The Falcons are playing the game under protest. It's something to be settled by the conference or by the state athletic association. It's nothing for us to worry about tonight. Okay?"

The players nodded.

"Now," she said, "the starters, same as before—Kovacs and Richardson at the forwards, Holcott at center, Cranston and Robinson at the guards."

She turned to Gary. "You'll see some action," she said.

Gary nodded. He was not surprised that he was not starting the game. After only one day of practice with the team, even Wilt Chamberlain probably would not have won a starter's role from Monica Conway. Gary turned and sat on the bench.

"Whipple! In for Kovacs!"

The game was five minutes old. The Pirates were leading Bennington by two points, 9–7.

At Monica's barked command, Gary leaped to his feet and ran to the scorer's table to check in.

From the start, with Gary sitting on the bench, the fans in the bleachers across from the bench had set up the chant: "We want Gary, we want Gary." Gary, grinning across at the crowd, spotted Howie Fenton, between Hubie Thompson and Raymo Bailey, leading the chant. When their eyes met, Howie put his forefingers in the sides of his mouth, pulled wide, and waggled his tongue at Gary.

Now, with Gary checking in at the scorer's table, a giant roar went up from the crowd, starting with the students around Howie and the other players and then spreading throughout the gymnasium.

Gary barely heard the cheer. His grin was gone. He was frowning. He stood motionless, staring at the action on the court, awaiting a break in the play to allow him to enter the game. As he watched the players on the court, he searched for one final confirmation: The Falcons did not, indeed, have the likes of Rita Cranston cavorting at guard, ready to steal the ball from his hands, and they did not have anyone to equal the terror of Frances Holcott at center. He was safe.

Then why were the palms of his hands sweating? He wiped his palms on the seat of his trunks.

On the court, an errant pass skittered off the outstretched fingers of a Bennington player and bounced out of bounds. In the break in the action, Gary trotted onto the court, reported his presence to the referee, and signaled Ruth to head for the bench.

The chant from the bleachers at the far side changed: "Go, Gary! Go, Gary! Go, Gary!"

Gary ignored the chant. He wiped the palms of his hands on the seat of his trunks again.

Debbie threw the ball inbounds to Rita. Rita dribbled easily to the center stripe. She circled around a defender and passed back to Debbie.

Gary backed toward the sideline and slid sideways

48

toward the corner. Debbie fired the ball inside to Frances. Frances, bottled up, pivoted. Suddenly the ball was coming at Gary. He put up his hands to take the ball. He worried about the sweat on his palms. No time to wipe them again. Then he had the ball. He held it. He dribbled once. The Bennington guard was playing too far off Gary, giving him a wide berth. She was probably facing a boy on the basketball court for the first time in her life. Shy, overly cautious, or whatever, she was leaving Gary wide open. Gary eyed the basket. He went up. He fired a soft, arching one-hander. The ball floated above the outstretched hands of the Bennington guard and swished through the net without touching the rim.

The crowd roared.

Gary, a wide grin on his face, shot a fist into the air in triumph.

The Bennington coach called a time-out.

At the end of the game the scoreboard read: Pirates 49, Falcons 33.

In the dressing room, Gary watched the last of the players on the boys' team—Horse Mueller, as luck would have it—depart for the court and the start of the boys' game.

"What a farce," Horse said with a scowl.

"Good luck to you, too," Gary piped to Horse's back going out the door.

Gary pulled off his uniform and stepped into the shower. He hardly needed the shower. He had played the three minutes at the end of the first quarter and four minutes late in the third quarter. And that was all. That was it, period. Otherwise he had sat on the bench and watched the game. He had scored eight points.

He reviewed his minutes on the playing court. There was no ducking the fact that he had found the going pretty tough in the third quarter. The clawing, double-teaming defense had bothered him. Those Bennington girls had learned pretty quickly how to keep their hands in his face. He beat them, to be sure, but they were a long way from the pushovers he had expected.

Still, he was bigger, quicker, more skilled than any of the girls on the Bennington team. He did not have to worry about sweaty palms any longer. He could handle what came along. And if some team down the road did have the likes of Rita Cranston or Frances Holcott. . . .

"Well," he told himself, "at least I won't be caught by surprise the way I was in that first practice session. Who would have thought . . . ?"

The embarrassing memory of the practice session faded. In its place came the exhilaration of his first scoring shot against the Falcons. Then the recollection of the chants from the crowd—first, "We want Gary," and then, "Go, Gary."

"It was fun," Gary said aloud and reached for the soap. He lathered, rinsed, and stepped out of the shower. He toweled off and walked to his locker, the towel around his waist even though he was alone in the room full of lockers and benches.

Once dressed, he stepped out of the locker room into the corridor. He waited a moment in the silence, and then he wandered toward the door to the girls' dressing room. He cocked an ear toward the dressing room. It was silent as a tomb. He wondered if the girls had already dressed and headed upstairs to watch the boys' game.

The door opened. Pamela, Debbie, and Rita came out together. Gary fell into step with Pamela.

"That doesn't sound much like the winners' dressing room in there," he said. "Is everyone always this morose, or are you just playing it cool?"

Rita, walking in front of Gary, turned and fixed a stern gaze on him. "It's not exactly as if we won, if you can understand what I mean." She turned and walked ahead of them down the corridor before Gary could answer.

Gary blinked. Then he managed a grin at Pamela. "Weird," he said.

The Madison High boys' team had better reason—statistically, at least—for a quiet dressing room. Raymo Bailey and Howie Fenton both fouled out midway through the fourth quarter, leaving the Pirates' forward line to substitutes. Horse Mueller committed his fourth foul at about the same time. Burdened with the danger of fouling out, he retreated into a cautious style of play and the Bennington center ran all over him. The end result was an upset 47–41 victory for the Bennington Falcons.

It was the Pirates' first loss of the young season.

Gary was seated among the somber spectators in the bleachers.

Chapter Six

The storm broke the next morning, and for three days it swirled around Gary, mostly out of his sight, mostly out of his earshot, but always there. The rumblings of the storm invariably found their way back to Gary. He was like a person who did not see the lightning bolt but heard the boom of the thunder coming after.

There were the meetings, one after the other, in George Gordon's office. The bustle of comings and goings was unusual. The business office of Madison High, with the principal's office off to the side, was normally a quiet place. People spoke in hushed tones. They went about their business at a leisurely pace, noiselessly. Few strangers ever walked through the door. When they did, they somehow felt the tone of the place immediately, and they adapted themselves to it. They walked softly, spoke quietly. But now streams of people, many of them strangers, were moving in and out. They did not walk softly. They did not speak quietly. They clattered through in twos and threes, intent on their own conversations. Occasionally their voices rose, producing a jarring, discordant note in the serene atmosphere of the business office at Madison High.

None of the activity escaped the attention of the students working at their clerical jobs: answering the telephone, filing, checking attendance records, helping with the typing. The students were all eyes and ears. And everything they saw and heard found its way out of the business office and into the corridors of Madison High while the student body went through the otherwise normal routine of pursuing an education.

The most eager of the listeners in the corridors was Gary Whipple. He wore a broad smile on his face. He nodded his head in excited acknowledgment of each new report. Gary Whipple was delighted. This had to be the most sensational caper of all time. He was pleased, very pleased.

The students working in the business office recognized the Madison High people coming and going: Orville Flynn, Mike Moseley, Monica Conway, and even the football coach, Hank Randefer. There were others, from outside the school, who were recognized as they came and went: a school-board member who had addressed the Madison High graduation ceremonies last spring, the well-known face of the executive secretary of the Illinois High School Athletic Association, and fresh from the memory of Tuesday night's game, the coach of the Bennington High Falcons girls' team. There were others, too, unrecognized, who filtered in and out of the business office.

The cluster of newspaper and television reporters, most of them from out of town, added to the growing appearance of chaos in the business office. George Gordon eyed the strange reporters nervously. Not knowing what else to do with them, he suggested they take seats, gesturing to a row of chairs normally reserved for boys and girls waiting to discuss their misbehavior with the principal.

"The school will have a statement," he told them.

The reporters sat down. But they stayed in the chairs only until the first recognizable face appeared in the doorway. Then they leaped up. They surrounded the startled visitor. They fired their questions. They kept firing their questions until the visitor finally made it to the safety of George Gordon's private office.

Then, on the way out, the visitor had to run the gauntlet, head down, ignoring the staccato questions.

Time and again the scene was replayed.

One reporter, more enterprising than the others, casually sauntered over to the counter and leaned over close to Amy Meredith. Amy was working as receptionist and answering the telephone.

"Could you tell me where Gary Whipple is in class at this moment?" he asked in a friendly manner.

The reporter had no way of knowing, but he had just run into Rule Number 1 of the business office of Madison High: Never give out the whereabouts of a student to a stranger.

Amy knew the rule. She smiled at the reporter. She excused herself. She walked across to the desk of Miss Margaret, the heart and the brain of the business office, and asked if she should comply. Miss Margaret glanced up at the reporter briefly. She looked at Amy. "No," she said.

The incident, like all the others, found its way into

the corridor grapevine. But a report of the incident also moved along official channels. And so it was that when Gary came out of algebra class, Monica Conway was waiting for him.

"Gary," she said, "there are reporters in the business office. They may try to question you. The smart thing for you to do right now is to say nothing."

Gary grinned at her. She seemed almost ready to return the smile. Gary remembered that he had always liked Monica Conway. She had always had a friendly word when she was waiting outside the dressing room for Mike Moseley. Gary liked her even more now. She really was nice. And he suspected that she might be enjoying the caper every bit as much as he.

Gary shifted his expression to a mixture of shock and disappointment. "Fame, it's mine," he said, "and you won't let me have it."

Monica did smile now. "We all have to make our little sacrifices," she said and walked away.

Across town, in the low red-brick building that housed the headquarters of the school district, the school board met, first on Wednesday afternoon and then on Thursday night.

At first the school board tried to meet behind closed doors. The Gary Whipple case was a problem that the school-board members preferred to tackle outside the glare of public view. But the reporters and television crews dogging their every step set up a howl. The school board was a public body, meeting to discuss public business, and the public was entitled to witness the proceedings. It was the law. The school board tried a ducking maneuver. The law allowed closed-door meetings for discussion of matters involving personnel. Gary Whipple was, everyone agreed, a person. So it was a personnel matter, and therefore the board members could meet in private. Yes, the reporters agreed, Gary Whipple was a person. But he was not an employee, and therefore discussion of his situation did not qualify as a personnel matter. Lawyers spoke on the telephone. The meeting was opened to the press and public.

Gary was tempted to attend the school-board meeting. "Now that might really be fun," he announced. While the tantalizing prospect raced through the corridor grapevine, and in addition, spilled out over the town, the Wednesday meeting came and went. Gary was in class until three-thirty. After that he had basketball practice.

Before he made up his mind about going to the Thursday night meeting, he found himself once again facing Monica Conway in the corridor outside a classroom.

She drew him to one side, away from the flow of the students changing classes. "Don't go," she said bluntly.

Gary grinned at her. She did not smile back.

"It's better that you don't go," she said.

"Aw," Gary said, screwing up his face in a mock pout, "I never get to have any fun."

Monica smiled slightly. "Life is just full of these little sacrifices, isn't it?"

As matters turned out, Gary did not miss much by

staying away from the school-board meeting. The sum total of the accomplishment of the two meetings was a pair of questions and a pair of answers: Question: Does the school district have a rule prohibiting boys and girls from playing on each other's teams? Answer: No. Question: Can the school board pass a rule now that would knock Gary Whipple off the girls' team and end forever his career as a girls' basketball player? Answer: No, not really, and probably for two reasons. One, any such rule would so obviously be aimed at the single person of Gary Whipple as to be discriminatory. And, two, there was heavy speculation that the proposal would not win the necessary majority vote anyway. Apparently some members of the school board felt that Gary Whipple was entitled to play on any team he chose at Madison High.

Outside Madison, at the headquarters of the Black Hawk Big Seven Conference, the result was the same—futile fumbling—although the scene was different.

Roy Marsh, the football coach of the Knightstown Eagles, happened to be serving his year in rotation as president of the conference. So the filing cabinet, which in fact was the headquarters of the conference, resided in his office in the basement of Knightstown High School.

Roy Marsh, unlike the school board, could close the door to reporters and television crews and the public, and he did.

But he could not stop the ringing of the telephone,

both in his office and at his home. He told all callers: "The Black Hawk Big Seven Conference does not have a rule prohibiting a boy from playing on a girls' team. I don't know if we ever will. I don't know if we should. I have no opinion. Good-bye."

Gary read in the newspaper the coach's statement, along with the coach's complaints about harassment. He heaved a sigh of relief. He smiled. He was still in action.

From Bloomington to the south, the Illinois High School Athletic Association's headquarters came forth with a statement. It was short and simple and— for the IHSAA, at least—an easy, comfortable, and painless statement: "This is not a problem for the IHSAA. It is a problem for the conference or for the school district." Period. End of statement.

Gary read that one with a smile, too. The caper was really flying.

For Gary, the three days before the Friday afternoon van ride to Lionel Falls for the Tigers' game sailed by.

During the day the routine of the classroom, spiced with the reports from the business office and the school board, kept Gary going at a fever pitch. He awoke each morning with an uncharacteristic eagerness to get himself to school. There was no telling what the day might bring. He looked forward to each class because when it was over there was the latest of the corridor gossip awaiting him.

All around him, his fellow students—and, it seemed, the teachers, too—were relishing each new development with the same fervor as Gary. He was having more fun than he could remember. So was everyone else.

Well, almost everyone.

There were exceptions. Clearly, George Gordon was not enjoying the sudden transition from tranquility to the edge of a hurricane. Orville Flynn, too, was not smiling when Gary saw him in the corridors. But maybe his mood was attributable to the loss at the hands of the Bennington Falcons. Mike Moseley looked angry, not amused. But Mike Moseley always looked angry. Horse Mueller barely spoke to Gary when they met, treating him as if he were a deserter or something like that. Rita Cranston, her mouth firmly set in a straight line, looked ready to explode every time she saw Gary.

Gary shrugged off the exceptions. In a world full of people, not everybody was going to enjoy having fun.

On Wednesday, at the first practice session following his surprise appearance against Bennington, the reporters and television crews swarmed around the court.

Monica Conway took one look at the assemblage and hailed them into a conference at the end of the court.

"Go ahead with your warm-ups," she told her players.

Everybody took their shots with one eye on the basket and one on the scene at the far end of the court. Monica was shaking her head and jabbing the air with her finger. Suddenly she turned and walked away from them, striding the half-length of the court toward her players, leaving the reporters and television crews huddled at their end of the court. As she crossed the center stripe, she gestured for the players to gather around her.

"Now hear this, and be certain you understand," she said. The players stood in a circle around her. Gary caught Pamela Hunt grinning at him and he smiled back at her. "Cut the grinning and listen to me," Monica said.

"I've told them that none of my players will be granting interviews." Monica paused. "You heard me—*none* will be granting *any* interviews. That means nobody answers any questions from reporters. Understood?"

She glanced around the circle of players. Some of them involuntarily nodded when their eyes met hers. When she came to Gary, she waited until he nodded, and then nodded back at him.

"I've agreed to give them ten minutes for pictures—the television crews and the newspaper photographers. After that, they're leaving. And they won't be back. I guarantee it."

Again she looked at Gary. He got the message: no horseplay.

For ten minutes, with bright lights on poles flooding one end of the court and with cameras whirring and clicking, the Pirates went through the normal paces of a warm-up drill: first, everyone taking long shots at the basket and following up for the rebound, and then a series of weaving patterns involving dribbling, handoffs, passes, and lay-up shots.

Then the bright lights on the poles went dark.

Somebody called out, "Thanks, Coach." And they left.

From that point, the order of the day was business as usual on the basketball court.

Chapter Seven

The boy, wearing the black-and-gold uniform of the Lionel Falls Tigers with number 12 on the back, did not join the girls on the court until the last moment.

The warm-up drills were past. The teams were gathering around their coaches at their benches flanking the scorer's table. The last words of advice were being issued.

"Oops," Gary said with a grin, gazing past Monica at the boy approaching the girls at the Lionel Falls bench.

Monica looked up and then turned to follow Gary's gaze. One by one, all of the Pirates turned and watched the boy joining the Lionel Falls girls' team at the bench.

All around the Lionel Falls gymnasium, packed with the Tigers' hometown fans, a murmur of startled conversation rolled down onto the court, then erupted into laughs, cheers, and applause. The Lionel Falls fans, like everyone else in the whole world, had heard about the Madison High girls' team player named Gary Whipple. They had hooted, laughed, and shouted at him during the warm-up drills. Now they were seeing their team's answer. They liked it. This was going to be fun.

Monica mumbled under her breath, "Uh-huh," as if she was not at all surprised. Apparently she had been expecting the development.

Gary recognized the boy. He had played against him last season. He did not know his name, but he knew he was a guard—a good one, quick, sure-handed, tenacious.

Monica turned back to her players. "Listen to me," she said quickly. "Play your own game. And—"

She got no further. The Tigers' coach was approaching down the sideline. Monica stopped in mid-sentence and turned to meet her.

"Hi, Monica," the Tigers' coach said with a smile. She was a friendly-looking woman, about Monica's age, a bit on the stout side, but with the fluid walk of an athlete. She wore a gold blazer over a black turtleneck sweater.

Monica extended a hand and returned the smile. "Hi, Betsy," she said. They shook hands.

"If you can, I can," Betsy said lightly, nodding her head toward the group of Lionel Falls players that included the boy. "Okay?"

"Of course," Monica said. She paused and then said, "But I've got just one question. Is your boy"—she gestured toward the Lionel Falls bench—"switching from the boys' team to the girls' team? Or is he expecting to play with both the girls' team and the boys' team?"

Monica paused again, letting the question and its implication sink in.

The Lionel Falls coach's easy smile faded slightly. The significance of Monica's question was written on her face.

Gary watched and listened in fascination. He knew what was coming. The plot was thickening.

Monica continued, "Gary Whipple has switched from the boys' team to the girls' team, and there is no rule prohibiting the switch. But there are rules—both conference rules and state athletic association rules—about players being active on two teams of the same sport, such as varsity and junior varsity. A player can't play on both. Presumably the same rule would apply to girls' and boy's teams."

The Lionel Falls coach listened without comment. The smile was completely gone. She was frowning. Then she shrugged and said, "We'll see." She turned and walked back past the scorer's table to her bench.

The referee was moving toward center court with the ball in his hand.

Monica turned to her players. "The starters—Holcott at center, Kovacs and Whipple at the forwards, Cranston and Robinson at the guards."

She threw Gary's name into the starting lineup without the slightest indication that anything unusual was happening. Her expression did not change. Her voice did not rise or fall.

Rita Cranston's expression changed. Gary was looking at her at the moment Monica spoke his name. Rita frowned. She clenched her jaw so tightly that Gary saw the muscle jump under the skin. She glanced at Gary. Their eyes met. Her eyes were flashing with anger.

Gary looked at Sharon Richardson. She was the player he had knocked out of the starting lineup. It was bound to be either Sharon or Ruth Kovacs, one of the forwards. Gary was bigger, stronger, and better than either of them. Gary wondered if Sharon, now staring at the floor, had known in advance. Surely she had. Surely Monica had told her.

"All right," Monica said, "let's go."

Gary, taking up his position for the tip-off, glanced around. The boy was not on the court with the Tigers. He was seated on the Lionel Falls bench, leaning back casually, watching without expression.

Maybe the Lionel Falls coach—Betsy what's-her-name—was having second thoughts about playing the boy. Betsy would not want to risk a forfeit by playing an ineligible player, which was what the boy might well turn out to be if he returned to the boys' team to play in the second game. And the coach of the Lionel Falls boys' team would not appreciate losing his star guard in the boys' game because he had played in the girls' game.

Gary grinned. The caper was sending reverberations all over the place.

The referee spun the ball into the air. The two centers—Frances and a lanky brunette with hair cropped shorter than Gary's—went up together. Gary abruptly ended his speculation about number 12 sitting on the Lionel Falls bench. He tensed his body and concentrated on the ball spinning upward.

Frances won the tip and flicked the ball to Gary's right. Gary sprang into the empty space and caught the ball. He dribbled twice and passed back to Rita while the Pirates moved into their offense positions.

Rita dribbled easily into position and passed back to Gary. Gary, without dribbling, turned quickly and

65

flung a high pass in the direction of Frances, now in front of the basket. Frances went up, hands reaching high. She turned. The lanky Lionel Falls center was with her, but too late. Frances patted the ball with her fingertips. The ball bounced off the backboard and dropped through the basket.

The scoreboard blinked—Tigers 0, Visitors 2—and the Pirates backpedaled to set up their defense.

For eight minutes, through the end of the first quarter, the two teams swapped goals, passing the lead back and forth. Through it all, number 12 sat on the Lionel Falls bench, now leaning forward, his elbows on his knees, hands clasped together, watching the action. When the buzzer ending the quarter sounded and the players trooped toward their benches, the score was 13–12 with the Pirates out front.

Monica wasted no time receiving her players at the bench. She told Frances to drop back under the basket. The lanky brunette was doing too good a job of stopping Frances' hook shots. Frances should be underneath the basket, ready for tip-ins like the one that got the Pirates their first field goal. Monica told Rita to drive for the basket more often. The little guard with the serious face was a sure-handed dribbler with above-average accuracy on lay-up shots. She might score some points. Also, her darting presence under the basket was sure to take some of the pressure off Frances.

As Monica spoke, Gary stared absently at Pamela Hunt. Monica's rapid-fire delivery of instructions was somewhere in the background, registering only in

Gary's subsconscious. Pamela smiled at Gary. Gary grinned back and winked.

"And you, Gary," Monica snapped suddenly. She was glaring at him. She had caught him mid-smile and mid-wink. "Are you with us, Whipple?"

Gary wiped the smile from his face. "Yes, sure."

Monica waited a moment. Then, as if nothing had happened, she said, "I want you to keep shooting. Your guard can't handle you. Let's play it for all it's worth. And one other thing. I'm moving Frances back under the basket. Send her some high passes."

"Right."

They turned to go back onto the court for the start of the second quarter. From somewhere in the crowd Gary heard his name. It was Howie's voice. Howie was shouting from somewhere up there in the bleachers. Gary turned to see if he could spot Howie. But Howie was not the one his eyes landed on. The furious glare of Kimberly Bennett, standing at the sideline with the cheerleaders, seemed to nail him in his tracks. For a second he gawked at her scowling face in puzzlement. Then he remembered. Yes, he had grinned and winked at Pamela. He remembered something else, too. Kimberly did not like him grinning and winking at other girls.

The boy wearing number 12 got off the bench with the second quarter barely a minute old. He shucked his warm-up jacket and dropped it on the bench. He walked to the scorer's table to register himself for action.

The noise of the crowd—first a wave of murmurs,

then a soft rumbling, and finally a wild burst of applause, whistles, and cheers—almost stopped the play on the court.

Gary had the ball. He was dribbling down the sideline. He heard the noise. He heard it erupt suddenly into a deafening sound. He knew what was happening. Then, out of the corner of his eye, he saw number 12 waiting at the scorer's table to enter the game. Gary turned and zipped a pass back to Debbie. A Lionel Falls player lunged toward the ball. She got a fingertip, but nothing more, on the ball. The deflected pass bounced off Debbie's hands and fell out of bounds.

Number 12 trotted onto the court, reported to the referee, and took up a position to receive the Lionel Falls pass inbounds.

The fans on both sides of the court were on their feet, roaring. Gary glanced at the scoreboard: Tigers 14, Visitors 17.

He glanced at the bench. He sought Monica's eye. The Pirates were facing a new and different threat. Did Monica want to switch from the Pirates' traditional zone defense to a man-to-man defense? He almost smiled at the thought. Man-to-man? Woman-to-woman? Maybe person-to-person? Yes, that was it. The funny sound of the term did bring a smile to Gary's face. Then his eyes met Monica's. She seemed to understand the question in his mind. She shook her head slightly. No, the Pirates would stick with their zone defense.

Number 12 took the pass inbounds and dribbled easily toward the center stripe, cutting across the court, away from Gary. Ruth moved over to intercept him. Number 12 crossed the center stripe and they met. He turned and passed the ball away, past the waggling hands of Ruth.

Gary pursued the girl with the ball. Ruth, stopping and starting, turning and whirling, tried to stick with number 12.

Two quick, short passes put the ball out of Gary's zone. Then a pass went back toward number 12, near the sideline, fifteen feet out from the basket. Ruth, turning, did not see the ball coming. Number 12 took in the pass behind Ruth's back. He dribbled away from Ruth, into Rita's zone.

Now he was facing the Pirates' best on defense. Rita, with her quick feet and her fast-moving hands, was the terror of any dribbler. Gary himself could testify to her abilities. This was, Gary was sure, going to be fun to watch—the confident boy dribbling without fear or suspicion into the lair of the deadly Rita Cranston.

Then Gary blinked in disbelief. He looked again. His eyes were not playing tricks. Rita, with the quick feet, was backing up, treading heavily, as if her feet carried lead weights. Rita, with the darting hands, was flailing her arms absently, almost in slow motion. She was giving ground. Instead of pressing the dribbler, she was backing away. Number 12 dribbled easily around her. Rita's final, frantic stab at the ball missed the mark by a foot. And he was gone.

Frances moved out to face him. Gary darted in behind Frances. He wanted to position himself for the rebound if number 12 got off a shot past Frances. He was sure to shoot. The look of a goal was in his eye. He was sure, also, to miss. Gary was certain of it. The first collision with Frances Holcott—a girl—was bound to come as a jolt to any boy, as Gary knew from personal experience. Number 12's shot, if not deflected by the leaping Frances, was going to be off the mark. It was going to be aimed wrong because of the surprise of Frances' physical impact. She was no soft, fluffy thing. Frances was sturdy as an oak and fearless.

Again Gary watched unbelievingly as Frances extended one arm upward, a rigid, ineffective barrier to the expected shot. She waved her other hand—tentatively, timidly—toward the ball.

Gary, seeing that Frances was fading in the face of number 12's drive toward the basket, tried to come around and intercept the dribbler. Gary stepped forward and reached around the right side of Frances. Number 12 cut and dribbled around the left side of Frances. Alone under the basket, with the unmoving Frances blocking Gary, number 12 laid up the ball. It rolled halfway around the rim and dropped in.

Gary, moving back downcourt to take up his offense position, watched Debbie step out of bounds for the throw-in. He saw Rita, hands extended, awaiting Debbie's pass. But the scene was a blur to Gary, overshadowed by the memory of Rita and Frances caving in, collapsing in the face of an intimidating boy player. Beyond him, downcourt, Gary saw Frances taking up her position. She appeared flustered, embarrassed.

Gary was astounded, and he was troubled. They

both, Rita and Frances, had handled Gary with dispatch in his first practice session with the girls' team. But apparently a boy they knew was one thing, and a stranger in another team's uniform was quite another. Apparently a practice session, with the bleachers empty, was one thing, and a game with two thousand onlookers was quite another.

Debbie threw the ball in. Rita took the pass. She turned and dribbled a couple of yards and then passed back to Debbie for the march over the center stripe. Only then did Gary recognize the hand waggling in front of his face—larger than any hand he had seen lately—and know that number 12 was tracking him.

Debbie fired a pass cross-court to Ruth, clearly intending to keep the ball away from number 12. Ruth, inexplicably, juggled the ball. Her guard, not ready to take advantage of an opportunity for a steal, failed to react. Ruth retained possession. Ruth swiveled on one foot, looking for a place to get rid of the ball.

Gary faked a darting movement to his left, screeched to a halt, leaped to his right, and left number 12 behind. Gary was free. Ruth sent a bounce pass—of all things, a bounce pass!—in Gary's direction. A straight pass fired into Gary's hands was a cinch for success. But a bounce pass took another second. In that second, number 12 recovered. He lunged in front of Gary and grabbed the ball.

By the time Gary set out in pursuit, the boy had heaved a high pass to the other end of the court. Two Tigers were racing under the ball. Rita ran after them. One of the Tigers pulled in the pass on the run.

71

Rita went after her. The Tiger dribbled once and passed across to her teammate. Rita wound up guarding the wrong Tiger. The Tiger with the ball laid it up for a field goal.

The roar from the crowd of Lionel Falls fans rolled across the court like ocean waves.

The scoreboard changed: Tigers 18, Visitors 17.

At the sideline, Monica Conway was stepping onto the court, her forearms forming a T, signaling for a time-out.

Trooping to the bench, Gary glanced at Frances and then at Rita. He knew that they, like the Bennington girl, had been told all their lives that boys were bigger, stronger, quicker, more skilled in athletics. In the crunch, they believed it. But it wasn't true. Rita could have—should have—tied number 12 in knots. Frances could have—should have—blasted number 12 out of the lane.

Monica stepped back and dropped to one knee as the players circled around her at the bench. She looked at the sweaty faces around her. Some of the players were toweling off. Some were staring at the coach. Others were looking at the floor.

"Cranston, you let that boy run over you," she snapped. She paused, glaring at Rita. The words went out like so many rifle bullets—bang, bang, bang. Rita turned red.

Monica turned to Frances. "Holcott, you let that boy knock you right out of the lane," she snapped. Frances, her freckled face blank, nodded slightly.

Gary shifted uncomfortably. He was embarrassed for the friend he liked to call Red. He was even embarrassed for Rita, despite all her angry glares.

He felt sorry for both of them, taking a verbal lashing in front of their teammates, in front of a crowd of spectators, and—perhaps worst of all—in front of Gary Whipple, a boy.

Monica was not finished. "Kovacs! How in the world can you explain a bounce pass in that kind of situation? Are you playing without your head? I thought I saw your head on your shoulders. If it's there, why don't you use it?"

Ruth kept her gaze on the floor. She shrugged her shoulders slightly.

"Look at me," Monica barked.

Ruth looked up.

"Did you hear me?"

The reply was faint, barely audible in the crowd noise: "Yes."

Monica glanced up quickly at the clock.

"Now listen to me carefully." Her voice was softer. She spoke in an advisory, almost conspiratorial tone. "You can whip that boy. You've got the skill, the quickness, and—yes—the strength to do it. A few minutes ago, when he ran over you, you didn't lack the skill or the quickness or the strength. You lacked the determination. You let him intimidate you."

For a brief moment, with a pang of alarm, Gary expected her to say: "Remember what you did to Whipple on the playing court the day of his first practice? Well, you can do the same to this boy."

But Monica's time was running out. "Now, you are going to go out there on the court and whip the boy because you can do it, or—" she paused, glancing at the faces around her—"or we will pack it in right now and quit and go home."

Gary glanced sharply at Monica. He was startled. He could not believe his ears. He never had heard such a challenge thrown down. Walk away and admit defeat? Quit?

"If you're going to quit, there's no point in playing out the rest of the game," she snapped. "If you've decided to quit, we can just pack it in and leave right now."

The anger in her eyes said as much as her words: she was not going to associate herself with a team that could not—or would not—battle for a victory.

"Well, which is it going to be?"

There was a moment of uncomfortable silence, broken finally by the referee's whistle summoning the players back to the court.

Another second of silence, with nobody moving.

"We'll whip 'em," Gary said softly. "All of 'em."

Chapter Eight

Number 12 did not take the court after the time-out. He was back on the bench, his warm-up jacket draped over his shoulders, sitting with his elbows on his knees, hands clasped together, staring straight ahead.

Gary looked around. By all rights, he and his teammates should be experiencing a great sense of relief in the absence of the boy. The big threat had been removed. The awesome power was gone. The Pirates were in a position to regain the lead, recapture the momentum.

But it wasn't that way. At this particular moment the Pirates needed the presence of number 12. They were ready to redeem themselves. They wanted to restore their self-confidence. They needed number 12 on the court to do it. Rita needed to beat him with her quickness. Frances needed to beat him with her strength. Gary wanted them to have him. The Pirates could not win back their self-confidence with number 12 sitting on the bench.

With a glance at the Lionel Falls bench, Gary wondered if the Tigers' coach knew how much the Pirates needed number 12 on the court. He wondered if this was an intentional move in the chess game of strategy the coaches always played from the sideline. Or, he wondered, was number 12 just getting a rest to save himself as much as possible for the boys' game?

Debbie's pass inbounds to Rita started the play and put an end to Gary's speculation.

Rita took the pass. She turned quickly. She started dribbling up the court. She was moving quickly, faster than usual. Her style was to dribble in an almost leisurely fashion toward the center stripe, sizing up the defense in front of her as she moved. But this time she fairly zipped toward the center line.

Debbie, coming up from behind, ran past Rita. Always, Debbie hung back, a safety valve for Rita, a place to send a pass if Rita encountered trouble. But this time she passed Rita and, looking back, gathered in a pass and dribbled across the center stripe.

Gary grinned at the change of pace. Without a word, Rita and Debbie had decided to redeem themselves, no matter whether number 12 was on the court or not. They didn't want to waste a second in making contact with the defense. They were eager for the battle.

Gary glanced over his shoulder at Frances. The big redheaded girl was moving around in front of the basket. Her eyes flashed a fury of intensity.

Okay, Gary thought, let's get them. Aloud, he shouted, "Run 'em, run 'em, run 'em."

At that moment, Debbie drilled a rifle shot of a pass into his hands. Gary turned and zipped a pass across to Ruth. Ruth sent it back to Gary, and Gary lofted a high pass in the direction of Frances. The redhead went up. She caught the ball on her finger-tips. She turned and —swish!

The Lionel Falls Tigers, Gary knew, had had their moment. Now they were in for a very tough evening—with number 12 on the court or without number 12 on the court—a very tough evening.

From there to the half time the Pirates clung to their slender lead—a lead of one point, two points, three points, then one point again—while number 12 remained on the bench.

"Fine, fine, good, good," Monica Conway was saying as she paced the floor of the dressing room at half time. She was speaking as Gary, having just knocked and entered after a brief intermission alone in the boys' dressing room, dropped onto a bench near the door.

"We'll see number 12 on the court again before this game is over, and you can bet on it," Monica said. "And we will play him just like any other player." She paused. "Any other player," she repeated. "I do not intend to pull Gary out of his assignment in order to guard the boy. That would give us four girls playing against four girls and one boy playing against one boy—ludicrous, and I won't have it. We're a team—five players on the court—facing another team, and that's the way we'll play. Got it?"

She was telling Frances that she had to beat the Tigers, the boy included. She was telling Rita that she had to beat the Tigers, the boy included. She was saying it to all of them.

As for Gary, he was pleased. If Frances and Rita and Debbie and the others could hold their own against the boy, Gary was more of an asset in his role. The Tigers, for their part, had assigned number 12 to guard Gary, which was a change in their basic system of defense. That could hurt the Tigers over the long haul of the second half.

In rapid-fire order Monica dealt out criticisms and instructions to the individual players. When she got to Gary: "Try to run number 12 as much as you can. Let's wear him out. It's the last thing the Tigers want to see. I'm betting they got the loan of him on the condition that he'd still be fresh enough to play in the boys' game. So make him pant and sweat when he's in there. Let's worry them. Okay?"

Gary grinned. The assignment was no problem. A boy who had dribbled on his knees knew how to run a guard ragged. It would be fun.

The intermission was running out. Monica glanced around the room. She seemed, without speaking, to be repeating the hard words at the sideline during the time-out: whip the boy or we'll just pack it in right now and go home.

Breaking the silence, Monica said, "All right, let's go."

When Frances and the lanky brunette and the referee gathered at the center of the court for the tip-off opening the second half, number 12 was on the court, standing next to Gary.

"Well, hello again," Gary piped.

Number 12 grinned at Gary a bit sheepishly.

"Great game we've got going here, huh?"

Number 12's grin widened a bit. He nodded.

The referee spun the ball into the air. Frances and

the lanky brunette went up. Again Frances won the tip. She flicked the ball away from Gary—and away from number 12—to an empty space to the left of Ruth. Ruth moved over and grabbed the ball, sending a quick pass to Rita. Rita dribbled easily, waiting for her teammates to position themselves for the attack.

Frances' chance to redeem herself against number 12 was not long in coming. She was bending, reaching for a low pass from Ruth. Number 12, trailing Gary, was nearby. When the pass from Ruth to Frances was in the air, number 12 turned from Gary and began a sweeping swing around Frances, hand extended, trying to deflect the ball. Frances, without even looking at him, swiveled a hip suddenly. Her sturdy hip, atop a strong leg, slammed into number 12's hip like a load of concrete. Running and reaching, number 12 was off balance when the blow hit. He almost fell. Frances caught the pass. She turned and began going up for her shot. Number 12, trying to regain his balance, leaned forward, catching Frances' elbow on his forehead. As if nothing had happened, Frances continued her smooth movement upward and laid the ball in the basket.

Number 12 staggered briefly. His eyes glazed over for a moment, and he shook his head jerkily from side to side.

Gary watched in fascination. There was no foul. Every one of Frances's moves had been legal under the rules. She shifted her hip to set herself for the leap to the basket. She accomplished the shift of the hip seconds before number 12 came around her side. If there was a foul, it was his, for charging. As for the elbow to the forehead, she was turning in her position—quite legally—when he inserted his head into the path of her elbow.

In any game, the one-two walloping would have been a stunner. It was no wonder number 12's knees buckled and his eyes went blank.

But in a game against a girl the two jolts had the extra punch of total surprise, which was the expression now written across the face of number 12. He eyed Frances in a funny way.

Gary, grinning at the spectacle of his nearby cock-eyed adversary, could not resist temptation. In the second before the resumption of play, he ran to number 12 and leaned in close to his ear. "Better watch her, she's tough," he said. And, with an expression of deadpan seriousness, "I have to be very careful in practice myself."

Number 12, unsmiling, stared back at Gary in silence. Thereafter, he approached Frances with noticeable caution.

Gary's role in handling number 12—wearing him out—took on added significance with each passing minute of the third quarter. Number 12 was clearly on the court to stay. Gary figured that the Tigers had hoped to ride the strength of number 12 to a comfortable lead in the third quarter, then let him sit out the fourth quarter, resting for the boys' game.

So Gary, every time he laid hands on the ball, dribbled in a crazy weaving pattern back and forth across the court. Number 12, in the jerky stop-start movements of the defender in pursuit, followed him.

By the end of the third quarter, Gary and number

12 were both panting and perspiring heavily, and the score was tied at 37–37.

Monica, receiving her players at the bench in the brief intermission, seemed satisfied. The Pirates had lost their one-point lead in the third quarter. The Tigers had outscored them by one point. But the Pirates had survived what obviously had been designed to be the Tigers' big push. The big push had not netted a big lead.

Gary, toweling off, was grinning. He was having fun. The look on number 12's face after Frances unloaded on him had to be one of the funniest sights of all time. And as number 12 chased Gary back and forth across the court, there was the growing realization—written all over his face—that Gary's assignment was to wear him out. Gary was wearing down, too, for sure. But Gary was not expected to play in a second game on this night.

Monica, talking to the players, stopped suddenly. She was gazing past the scorer's table, in the direction of the Tigers' bench. The players turned their heads and followed her gaze. Gary recognized the man talking to the Tigers' coach. He was the coach of the boys' team. He was doing the talking. The coach of the girls' team was nodding. Then the coach of the boys' team walked away.

"We've seen the last of number 12," Monica said. Before anyone around her could speak, she added, "But make no mistake, this is still one tough game. The score is tied. The Tigers are good—maybe better without number 12."

Monica was right. From the opening second, the

fourth quarter was a frantic, desperate scramble. To Gary the scene around him on the court reminded him of a movie with the projector turned to high speed. The players—all of them, on both teams— were moving at double time. There was fierce clawing for the ball. The guarding was tighter than ever. The battle for rebounds was brutal.

Early in the going, Gary felt the results of the merry chase he had led for number 12. He was winded. His arms were heavy. His legs had little spring left in them. Monica pulled him from the game for a few minutes of rest on the bench. Sharon Richardson took his place. He returned to the game after three minutes.

Never were the teams separated by more than two points.

With one minute remaining on the clock, with the score tied at 48–48, the Tigers brought the ball downcourt and sent a pass rifling in to the lanky brunette under the basket. Frances swarmed over her. The tall girl, pivoting in an effort to escape Frances, suddenly faced Debbie. Debbie grabbed the ball out of her hands. Instantly, Debbie was surrounded. Then, for reasons nobody knew, the whole crowd tumbled to the floor, the ball rolling out of bounds.

Last up was Debbie, holding her knee. She limped off the court, and Pamela Hunt jogged in to replace her.

The referee ruled that the ball was last touched by a Tiger, giving the Pirates the out-of-bounds throw-in.

Pamela stepped out of bounds, took the ball from

the referee, tossed it to Rita, and joined in the race upcourt.

The seconds were ticking away on the clock. Forty of them—just forty seconds—left to play. The noise from the crowd was deafening. They had booed the collision under the basket, wanting a foul to be called on one of the Pirates. Then they had booed the out-of-bounds ruling that gave the Pirates possession of the ball. Now they exhorted their Tigers to steal the ball and score and win the game.

Rita brought the ball across the center stripe.

The upcoming play—so very important—was obvious to all, Pirates and Tigers alike: Rita passing to Gary and Gary sending a high pass to Frances for the tip-in goal to win the game.

The Tigers double-teamed Gary. They sent a second player in to bottle up Frances. Rita, seeing what was happening, passed to the wide-open Ruth. Pamela cut across, trying to draw one of the defenders off Gary. It didn't work. They stuck to Gary. They allowed Pamela to move through unhindered. Ruth passed to Pamela. Pamela, all alone with the ball at the side of the court, gave Frances a quick glance. The two Tigers had Frances tied up under the basket. Pamela looked at Gary. He was surrounded by the four arms of the two girls guarding him. Pamela did not hesitate. She pumped an arching shot toward the basket. The ball floated, dropped, and—swish—fell through the basket.

Gary, running in a wide semicircle trying to elude his two guards, came under the basket as the ball dropped through. He was there to fight for the rebound if the shot had missed. He grabbed the ball, and with a loud whoop slammed the ball to the floor, and ran on toward Pamela. He grabbed her in a giant bear hug. The buzzer sounded, ending the game, just as he lifted her off her feet and whirled her around.

Over her shoulder he saw Kimberly. She was the only cheerleader who was not leaping and shouting. Kimberly was standing flatfooted, hands at her sides, glaring daggers at Gary.

"Oops," Gary said, lowering Pamela till her feet touched the floor.

Chapter Nine

By the time Gary showered and dressed and made his way upstairs to the court, the boys' game was in its fifth minute of play. Gary looked at the scoreboard. The Pirates were leading the Tigers 6–4. He scanned the court for number 12, then located him on the bench. Gary grinned. "Still breathing hard, huh, fella," he mumbled to himself. The thought occurred to Gary that maybe Mr. Flynn owed him one for exhausting an opponent before a game. He knew he would never deliver the wisecrack to Mr. Flynn.

He spotted Kimberly among the cheerleaders sitting cross-legged on the floor next to the scorer's table. He stared at her for a few minutes. Finally she felt his gaze and turned. He waved at her. She jerked her head back around and resumed staring at the play on the court without acknowledging his wave.

Gary lifted an eyebrow. For the first time, he sensed the seriousness of Kimberly's objections. She was really miffed. Those frowns had been the real thing. Gary caught himself frowning at the thought. He had not planned on trouble with Kimberly. Well, he would have a talk with her. Not now, not alongside the court during a game. But later, at the dance back at Madison High. Plenty of time to talk then. He could fix things up.

Across the way, near the front door to the gymnasium, he saw his teammates—the girls of the Madison High team—standing in a group. They were below the section of seats set aside for the Madison High fans accompanying the Pirates on the short trip to Lionel Falls. Pamela, fairly aglow, was the center of the activity. She was smiling and shouting to the fans and then cupping her hand to her ear to catch their replies. The hero of the game, the scorer of the winning field goal, was enjoying herself. For Pamela, who seldom saw game action much less gained the hero's role, it was a rare treat.

Gary began working his way around the edge of the court toward the girls.

The Lionel Falls fans recognized him. "Hey, there's one of the Madison girl players now," somebody shouted. "Yeah, ain't he sweet!"

Gary responded with a smile and a wave and kept threading his way toward the other end of the court.

Frances spotted him approaching and smiled.

"Hi-ya, Red," Gary said. "You played a great game."

"Thank you."

"I would have told you in the dressing room, but, well, you know how it is."

She grinned at him.

Gary joined the group. From behind he heard the words, "Good game." He turned and, to his surprise, found himself looking down into the face of Rita Cranston. "You really did," Rita said. She wore a serious expression, not the usual flare of anger, but simple seriousness. She spoke softly. "You held together when the rest of us were . . . well, you know . . . falling apart."

Gary, for the first time in memory, was speechless. He gaped at her, unable to find words. Was this really Rita Cranston? Hard-eyed, taut-jawed, angry li'l ol' Rita? It could not be. He stared at her in silence.

"I think we all learned something out there tonight," she said. "I know I did."

Gary found his voice. "I learned something, too," he said. "You and Frances and . . . and all of you are pretty tough basketball players."

Above them in the bleacher seats, the Madison High fans began squeezing together to make room for the players to take seats. Gary climbed up with the rest of them and dropped into a seat. Only as he was settling into his seat did he notice that Pamela was seated next to him.

"Oops," he said aloud.

"What?" Pamela asked.

"Nothing," Gary said with a grin. "Nothing at all."

On the court, one of the teams had called a time-out. The players were at their benches, standing around their coaches. As always during a time-out, the cheerleaders bounded up and scampered onto the court to lead a cheer. They always did. But Gary could not testify as an eyewitness on this occasion. He was staring down at his feet, wishing the time-out would end and Kimberly would have to move back to the sideline, out of her position in front of him.

The clock showed five minutes left to play. The scoreboard read 54–50 in favor of the Pirates. The Lionel Falls Tigers, always tough, were battling with every effort to knock off the perennially favored Pirates. An upset victory would be great. The Pirates had reasons of their own to want to win. They had lost last time out. Not in ten years had the Pirates lost two in a row. They were determined not to let it happen tonight.

Gary, leaning forward, elbows on his knees, chin resting on his fists, watched the action.

Howie, taking a pass in the corner, drove for the basket. Howie was good at driving for the basket. He had a peculiar wobbling style of dribbling. It was deceptive. Was he dribbling to the right? Was he going left? Nobody could tell. This time, he headed straight for the Lionel Falls center, who was standing his ground in front of the basket. Howie went up. The center held his position. Howie bumped his shoulder. The ball dropped through the hoop.

But the referee's whistle sounded immediately. As he blew the whistle, the referee waggled his hands, palms down. No goal—foul.

Howie ruefully raised a hand to identify himself to the scorer as the culprit, and turned and walked off the court. The foul was Howie's fifth. He was out of the game.

Hubie Thompson trotted onto the court to replace Howie.

Gary glanced at the clock again. What the Madison High Pirates needed at this moment, with Howie fouling out, was not Hubie Thompson replacing him. Hubie, a decent enough shot from the outside, was a little on the slow side, a slightly uncertain ball handler, and a poor dribbler. What the Pirates needed, Gary knew, was Gary Whipple. This was the moment to slow down the pace of the game. This was the time to control the ball. This was the time to eat up the seconds and minutes on the clock, take only the sure shots, and coast to the finish in victory. Horse Mueller had four fouls, rendering him overcautious. The Pirates were in dire trouble if their big center fouled out. So the logical strategy called for a maximum of fancy dribbling at mid-court and a minimum of roughstuff scrambling for a rebound under the basket. The situation was tailor-made for the talents of Gary Whipple.

This game was the second in a row in which Howie had fouled out. In the last game—and in this one—Howie had logged more playing minutes on the court and less rest on the bench than usual. The Pirates did not have their strong sixth man, Gary Whipple, on the bench to spell Howie. Orville Flynn was reluctant to pull Howie out of the game when the replacement was Hubie Thompson.

The Lionel Falls center scored on his free throw. The score was 54–51. The time remaining was just under five minutes.

Gary turned his head and looked at the Madison High bench. Howie, his shoulders covered with his warm-up jacket, was sitting forward, staring at the floor. Mike Moseley was on his feet, waving an arm and shouting something to Raymo Bailey. Raymo could not hear Mike Moseley over the noise of the crowd. The Lionel Falls fans now sensed that victory was within the grasp of their Tigers. Mr. Flynn sat easily on the bench, arms folded and legs crossed. He

89

could have been on a park bench in the springtime, watching the pigeons.

On the court, the Pirates brought the ball across the center stripe. Raymo and Hubie at the front and the two guards at the back settled into a pattern of passing the ball around the perimeter of the Lionel Falls defense.

Gary again thought a dribbler, such as Gary Whipple, was needed. A dribbler would eat up more time than passers tossing the ball around. Gary could dribble forever at mid-court—until the defense moved out to chase him, opening up the middle for a score. Using a dribbler would be less risky than having passes floating through the air, unprotected. At any moment a lunging Tiger might spear the ball and head for the open court.

And that's what happened. Raymo, with the ball, turned casually—too casually, as it turned out—and sent a soft pass to the guard to his right. A Lionel Falls player leaped forward at the moment the ball left Raymo's hand. Raymo realized his mistake too late. The Lionel Falls player got a hand on the ball, enough somehow to gain control. He and the ball came perilously close to going out of bounds. But he kept his feet inside the stripe and brought the ball down between his feet. He cut back toward the center of the court, eluding a charging Madison High player, and homed in on the basket. There was nothing but empty space between him and a field goal. He laid the ball up and it fell through.

The score was 54–53. A little over three minutes remained on the clock.

The noise in the gymnasium was deafening. The

Tigers on the court were leaping and shouting and clapping each other on the back. The Tigers at the bench were on their feet shouting. The Tiger who had scored on the lay-up was mobbed under the backboard by fans standing at the end of the gymnasium. The Pirates, for their part, looked deflated. Raymo avoided looking at the bench. He did not need either the quiet reproach of Orville Flynn or the fiery anger of Mike Moseley. Raymo knew his mistake. Horse Mueller's face was a study in frustration. The big center's four fouls had forced the strategy in the backcourt that set up the interception.

Having led since the early minutes of the second quarter, the Pirates now found themselves in danger of losing.

For Gary, sitting in the bleachers, an odd thought danced through his mind as he watched the wild scene before his eyes. How long, he wondered, had Mr. Flynn planned to keep him under suspension? One game? If only one game, he would have been out there on the court at this moment. He would have been playing tonight. Gary shrugged and turned his attention back to the play on the court.

The Pirates were putting the ball back into play, moving down the court, setting up their semicircle of players around the Tigers' defense.

But this time there was no lackadaisical passing. There were no casual tosses. This time more was needed than ticking the seconds off the clock. The Pirates needed a field goal. They needed a field goal right now. The passes zipped crisply around the semicircle, the Pirates looking for an opening.

Suddenly Raymo broke from his station and ran toward the goal. Hubie shot a pass at the empty space in front of Raymo. Raymo took in the ball. He dribbled once. He went up. The Lionel Falls defense went up with him. But Raymo did not shoot. He dropped the ball off to Horse. With the defense following Raymo, Horse was alone. He put the ball into the basket.

In the remaining three minutes the Pirates added a free throw and won the game 57–53.

Gary stood up with the rest of the crowd. He saw Kimberly and the other cheerleaders dance to the center of the court for one last cheer in victory. Around Gary, the cluster of Madison High fans sent up the only sound in the gymnasium. The Madison High Pirates had won. The Lionel Falls Tigers had lost.

Orville Flynn trailed his players off the court at the other end of the gymnasium. They disappeared through the door leading to the dressing room.

Moving slowly down the rows of bleacher seats with the fans, Gary saw Monica Conway standing at the front door, watching for her players. Beyond her, he saw Kimberly and the cheerleaders filing out the door, heading for their station wagon and the ride back to Madison. He would see Kimberly at the dance back at Madison High.

In the team van, with Monica at the wheel, Gary sat in the front seat, between Monica and Pamela Hunt, staring through the windshield into the darkness, hardly saying a word during the thirty-minute drive.

Chapter Ten

The van carrying the girls' team arrived back in Madison with the stream of cars carrying the students and fans. Somewhere in the line of cars was the station wagon carrying Kimberly and the other cheerleaders. The boys' team, having to shower and dress before boarding their van, would be thirty minutes behind.

Gary stepped out of the van and walked across the darkened parking lot toward the lights of the gymnasium. He could hear the electronic blaring of the combo. Shadowy figures were moving through the door. To his left, somebody said, "Nice game." He could not recognize the person in the darkness. He replied, "Thanks."

Gary walked through the door into the bright lights of the gymnasium. Frances Holcott followed him in and cut toward the concession counter to their right.

"See you later, Red," Gary called out.

"Yeah."

He stepped inside, out of the door, and scanned the room, now filling rapidly. Students were three deep around the concession counter. In the center of the floor several couples gyrated to the reverberating rhythm of the combo. Others stood around the edges

93

of the floor. He finally spotted Kimberly. She was on the other side of the gym. She was standing with Barbara Sharpe, who was waiting for Howie to arrive on the boys' team van. They were chatting with a couple of other cheerleaders. Gary began walking toward her and, when she looked at him, he waved and smiled.

"Hi," he said. "How goes it?" He nodded to Barbara and to the other girls. He turned back to Kimberly.

Without a word, Kimberly turned and walked around him and away.

Gary looked at Barbara.

"You have a problem, Dr. Whipple," she said.

"Uh-huh," he said. He followed Kimberly. "What's eating you?"

Kimberly stopped and turned, facing him. "I'm surprised to see you—" she paused for emphasis "—alone!"

"What do you mean—alone?"

"You know what I mean."

"Aw, c'mon—"

"Aw, c'mon yourself," she snapped. "You were making goo-goo eyes at Pamela. It got so bad that Coach Conway had to tell you to stop. I saw it all. You were hugging her, right out there on the court in front of everybody. I saw it. You were sitting next to her in the bleachers. I saw it. Do you think I'm blind?"

"Aw, Kimberly—"

"You probably sat next to her in the van coming home, too."

Gary's jaw dropped.

"You did!" she announced with a note of triumph.

"Good grief!"

"I'm going home," Kimberly said. "I don't like this party."

With that, she turned and walked out of the door, leaving Gary standing alone near the free-throw line.

Dumbfounded, Gary gawked into space until the space, suddenly, was filled with the leering face of Howie Fenton.

"Well, admit it," Howie said. "You did make goo-goo eyes at Pamela. You did hug Pamela. You did sit next to her. C'mon, admit it."

"Where did you come from?"

"Lionel Falls." Howie grinned. "I played in a basketball game over there tonight. Our boys' team played right after the girls' game."

"Go jump in the lake."

"I play for the boys' team," Howie continued. "We won."

Gary turned on him. "You fouled out, and you darned near got whipped."

Howie turned somber. "Yeah," he said. "We really could have used you out there tonight."

"I wonder if she really went home," Gary said, glancing around the gymnasium.

"You can bet on it," Howie said. "And I know another one that will be going home in a huff if I don't get over there and do my duty."

Gary watched Howie head for the sideline where Barbara was waiting with the two cheerleaders.

For almost half an hour Gary wandered around the

gym. He bought himself a Coke. He visited with Frances Holcott. He spotted Pamela and ducked the other way. The last thing he needed, for sure, was for Kimberly to hear he had been with Pamela. He ran into Mike Moseley and Monica Conway, casually at work at their chaperone assignments. He nodded and kept going. He saw Rita Cranston. He started to approach her and find out if the new Rita was really different. Then he thought better of it. He turned away. He bumped into Raymo and congratulated him on the spectacular play that set Horse up for the game's final field goal.

Finally he decided that he might as well go home himself. These things weren't any fun if he wasn't hanging around with the usual gang. And tonight, without Kimberly, he was a fifth wheel with the usual gang. He walked out the door into the night.

From there the weekend got no better for Gary.

"Where's Kimberly?" Gary's mother asked.

The hour of their usual Saturday morning tennis date had passed with Gary wandering aimlessly around the house. Lunch had passed with no mention of plans—maybe an afternoon visit to the record store in the mall with Kimberly, perhaps a movie in the evening with Kimberly.

"I don't know," Gary said.

"Did you call her?"

"She won't come to the phone."

"Oh."

Gary knew what was on Howie's mind the instant he heard the horn honk and turned to see the familiar red Jeep pull up to the curb. Gary was raking leaves in the front yard. Howie beeped the horn again and waved, gesturing for Gary to join him. Gary dropped the rake and walked to the Jeep.

"Hey," he said.

"Hey," Howie replied. "Hop in."

"I've got to finish the leaves."

Howie looked at the yard. "You're almost done."

"My dad doesn't think that almost is enough."

Howie glanced at the yard again. He seemed to be measuring what was left to be done. "C'mon, I'll help," he said. "You rake and I'll bag 'em and carry 'em, and we'll be finished in a jiffy."

"That's a deal I can't refuse."

They headed for the pile of leaves.

"Where we going?" Gary asked as he raked the last scattering of leaves into the pile, and Howie scooped them up in a huge armful for the bag.

"Nowhere."

"Okay."

In five more minutes they were roaring away from Gary's house in the red Jeep.

"You talk to Barb today?"

"Yeah, why?"

"She say anything about Kimberly?"

"Sort of."

"Sort of?"

"Kimberly is not real happy with you these days."

"She won't come to the phone."

"You know, she didn't dig this business of you switching to the girls' team from the start."

"She always liked a laugh."

"Well, this one is different."

97

"I don't see—"

Howie laughed. "For one thing, if you're going to hug a teammate, it'd better be Frances or Ruth—or anybody—instead of Pamela Hunt."

"Uh-huh."

There was a moment of silence as they drove along, and then Howie said, "I'll bet everything would be fixed up right away if you came back to the boys' team."

Howie's statement, and the way he spoke the words—almost as if he had rehearsed the line— caused Gary to give him a sharp glance. "Did Barb tell you that Kimberly said that?"

"Not exactly."

"Doesn't matter."

"What do you mean?"

"I don't have to ask Kimberly's permission to do anything."

In the silence that followed, Gary felt a vaguely troublesome thought nagging at the back of his mind. He had felt it first when he sat in the bleachers and watched the Pirates lose to Bennington. He had felt it again when he saw Howie foul out in the closing minutes of the game the night before. Now the feeling returned with the word that somebody—in this case, Kimberly—felt Gary was in the wrong place, whatever the reasons.

"You know, we really needed you last night," Howie said, turning onto the Lake Jackson road and wrestling with the stick to shift into second gear.

Gary sighed and stared straight ahead through the Jeep's windshield. Here it comes, he told himself, the big pitch from Howie. He had expected it the instant he heard the beeping of the Jeep's horn in front of his house. He didn't know how to answer Howie. He had caught himself searching for the answer in the darkness on the drive back to Madison. He had looked for the answer during the slow walk home from the party in the gymnasium. He had searched in the leaves he was raking. But he hadn't come up with an answer.

He wished the troublesome thoughts in the back of his mind would go away.

Gary said nothing, letting the flat countryside between town and Lake Jackson roll by. Howie shifted back into high gear.

"Hubie's okay, I guess, but—"

"Did Mr. Flynn send you?" Gary asked the question just to knock Howie's big pitch off stride for a moment.

Howie took his eyes off the road and looked at Gary. "You already know the answer to that one," he said.

"Yeah," he said with a half grin. He did know the answer. Mr. Flynn would never—not ever—ask a player to return to his team. In Mr. Flynn's book, it was up to the player to do the asking. Always. Mr. Flynn would not ask the greatest player in the world to come back, much less a bench warmer who had departed under the shadow of a disciplinary suspension.

"We need you," Howie said suddenly. "I mean, like really."

Gary said nothing.

"We lost one game, and then we darned near lost

99

another one," Howie continued, "and all because we didn't have the strong sixth man—you."

"I was suspended," Gary said flatly.

"Well, we were talking about that—Raymo and Hubie and Horse and me—in the van coming back last night."

"Horse!"

"Yeah." He paused. "Aw, c'mon, Horse is okay. A little weird, but okay."

"Okay."

Howie slowed the Jeep and shifted down for the last curve before the end of the road and arrival at Lake Jackson. The Jeep jerked when the gears changed and pulled up the slight incline to the top of the hill overlooking the lake. Howie braked to a halt. Below, the beach was empty and the concession stands were shuttered. The place was deserted.

"We think that if you went to Mr. Flynn, and if you asked him to let you come back, and if you promised no more of the monkey business, then—"

Gary tuned Howie's voice out. He remembered his somber feelings when the Pirates lost the Bennington game for the lack of a strong player coming in off the bench. He remembered how he had felt when the Pirates teetered on the edge and almost fell to Lionel Falls just the night before, for the same reason.

Maybe the caper had run its course. After all. . .

Then he stopped himself. The caper had not run its course. The caper was still fun. Besides, who was to say the Pirates would have whipped Bennington if Gary Whipple had been available? The Pirates had lost before with Gary playing. And against Lionel

100

Falls, well, the fact was that the Pirates won the game. They won it without Gary Whipple. Maybe Gary at first, and now Howie, tended to make too much of Gary's value to the Pirates. Orville Flynn knew better. He had suspended Gary from game action. So why not ride a caper that was still fun? Who was to know what would happen next? Who was to know where it would lead?

Gary interrupted Howie's monologue. "It wouldn't be much fun," he said. "It sounds dull."

"Dull, coming back to the team? Fun? What are you talking about?"

"You know."

"Look, a gag is a gag, but after all."

"I'll think about it," Gary said. "Okay?"

Howie stared at him for a moment. Then he said, "Okay," and turned the key to start up the Jeep for the ride back.

Chapter Eleven

Over the weekend, even without Kimberly, there were plenty of laughs—wisecracks in the Pirates' Den, cheers for the way Gary had forced number 12 to run out of gas, jokes of warning about the Lambert Hornets coming up on Tuesday night.

And when school resumed on Monday, the caper was rolling strong. The principal's office was going wild. The school board was up in the air. The conference headquarters over at Knightstown was in a tizzy. The reports from everywhere rippled through the corridors of Madison High.

Rumors were flying that the conference, in the person of the beleaguered Roy Marsh, was going to file suit. He was going to ask a court to throw Gary off the Madison High girls' team on grounds of—well, nobody knew quite what.

Clearly, Roy Marsh was being hammered from all sides with all kinds of demands for all kinds of action. Voices from all directions were screaming that he do something—anything.

The Bennington coach's protest, including a demand for a forfeiture, remained on his desk, untouched. At every opportunity the Bennington coach reminded the world that Roy Marsh had not acted. The Lionel Falls coach, having gone down to defeat in her scheme to send number 12 after Gary, also was making a demand. She was demanding that the conference declare the game null and void—in effect, never played. She wanted a rescheduling of the game, with Gary sitting in the bleachers where he belonged and her number 12 sitting there with him.

Even Monica Conway and Orville Flynn delivered a demand upon Roy Marsh. In a letter signed by the both of them, they protested the appearance of number 12 in both a girls' game and a boys' game on the same night. Her Pirates having won, Monica, of course, did not call for a forfeit. Neither did Mr. Flynn, with his boys' team having won also. But they both had an eye on the future, when their teams might come up losers. They called on the conference president to restate publicly the rule prohibiting athletes from playing on two teams at the same time. After all, they pointed out, Gary Whipple was a member of the girls' team and no longer a member of the boys' team.

As the protests flowed toward Roy Marsh's desk, Gary detected a gradual calming of the storm at the school board and in the administrative offices of Madison High. The arguments among the school-board members seemed to subside. The steady stream of people moving in and out of George Gordon's office slowed to a trickle. Even the visits of Orville Flynn and Monica Conway for closed-door conferences in Mr. Gordon's office fell off to nothing. Everyone, it seemed, had decided that the problem indeed did belong to the Big Seven Black Hawk Conference. Everyone was content to settle back and see what happened next.

And what happened next was that women started coming after Roy Marsh. Not the women coaches. Not the women members of the school board. Not the women teachers and the women administrators of the schools in the area. The women attacking Roy Marsh were housewives. They were mothers. They were secretaries. They were real estate saleswomen. They were clerks in stores, managers of shops, the whole spectrum of society, female gender. It seemed there were a million of them.

Gary watched and read and listened in fascination. To be sure, he had heard of the women's liberation movement. Everyone had. His father called them "libbers" and didn't seem to think much of them. As for Gary himself, he did not enjoy the likes of Rita Cranston's antagonism toward boys. But he figured, how can anyone be against equal rights, equal pay for equal work, equal opportunity, and all that? With a shrug, he decided he would qualify as a "libber" in his father's book.

But now it turned out that there was more involved than the one word *equality* when it came to arguing about women's liberation. One woman's equality, it seemed, was another woman's inequality.

From the capital at Springfield, the state headquarters of one of the women's groups issued statements demanding that Roy Marsh immediately ban Gary from the girls' team. They suggested, too, that Roy Marsh should ban Gary from *all* sports, the boys' team included. It would, they said, be a fitting punishment for the violator of the girls' rights to have a basketball team. Also, they said, it would serve as ample warning to any other troublemaker toying with the idea of gate-crashing the rightful domain of girl athletes.

Roy Marsh declined comment.

Gary did not decline comment. "They forgot to mention public flogging," he said.

The wisecrack got a laugh. But Gary, with the laughter of his friends still ringing in his ears, thought of Sharon Richardson, now riding the bench because Gary had joined the girls' team. Gary was frowning by the time the laughter was dying away.

Another women's group, to Gary's surprise and amazement, hailed him as a hero. He was a pioneer carving out exciting new trails in the quest for equality of the sexes. He was leading the way to total integration. He was showing the way to the end, finally, of sex discrimination. What was needed from Roy Marsh, they said, was a resounding endorsement of Gary's shattering of the ancient barriers.

Gary remembered Monica Conway's statement. She favored *one* varsity team, composed of the best players, be they boys or girls. She had not been kidding.

Again Roy Marsh declined comment.

So did Gary, this time, when the women's group wound up the statement by calling on Frances Holcott to take the second significant step toward equality by joining the boys' team. Gary blinked at the thought. Orville Flynn's Pirates with a girl in the lineup! A couple of minutes passed before the other side of the proposition appeared to Gary: Monica Conway's Pirates with a boy in the lineup! Again Gary frowned.

Three times on Monday night the telephone rang in the Whipple household for Gary.

The first caller, a courteous lady, identified herself—the name meant nothing to Gary—and then proceeded to explain in long, boring detail the harm Gary was doing. Most girls, she said, could not compete with boys in basketball. If there were no teams confined to girls only, the girls would not be able to play. Gary mumbled, "Yes, ma'am," a half-dozen times, and she finally quit talking and hung up.

The second caller was not long and boring. She was not courteous, either. She told Gary that he needed a sound thrashing and slammed the telephone down in his ear.

The third caller was Monica Conway. "I'm getting telephone calls at home," she said, "and I suppose you're getting them, too."

"A couple."

"Don't say anything, nothing at all. Understand?"

"I'll be as quiet as Roy Marsh," Gary quipped.

There was a moment of silence on the line. Then Monica said, "All right."

The wisecrack about Roy Marsh had popped out almost automatically. But Gary was not smiling. Increasingly, he seemed to find more to frown about than to laugh about.

Kimberley was not speaking to him. On Monday morning, and again on Tuesday morning, he showed up before classes at the spot in the lobby where they always met to start the day. She did not appear on Monday. She did not appear on Tuesday.

In the two classes they had together—advanced algebra and German—Kimberly arrived at the last minute. Looking neither left nor right, she marched to her seat. At the end of class she got to her feet and walked briskly out the door, turning the opposite direction from the path she knew Gary had to take to his next class.

The few times they met in the corridors, Kimberly put her nose in the air and marched past without looking at him. Once Gary saw her walking with Horse Mueller. As he stood there gawking, she was chattering and laughing. Even Horse was smiling.

Gary scratched his head. What was so bad about smiling at Pamela Hunt? Plenty, apparently. What was wrong with hugging a teammate who'd just shot the game-winning field goal? Plenty, it seemed, if the teammate happened to be Pamela Hunt. What was so bad about sitting—first in the bleachers, then in the team van—next to Pamela Hunt? Plenty.

Pamela herself was not smiling. "Kimberly won't speak to me," she blurted at Gary. "And she's supposed to be my best friend."

"Welcome to the club," Gary said. He was not smiling at Pamela now.

Howie and Hubie and Raymo and the rest of the members of the boys' team were increasingly cool toward Gary. No longer did any of his former teammates automatically follow him to his table in the cafeteria at lunchtime. He had to seek them out. And when he sat with them, there wasn't much laughter. No longer did they wave and shout at him in the corridor and laugh. The caper no longer amused them.

Undoubtedly Howie had wasted no time reporting his conversation with Gary at Lake Jackson to the team. They needed Gary back on the team. They all knew it. But Gary wasn't coming back, and they knew that, too.

Well, Gary told himself, the first game he missed—the Pirates' loss—was not his fault. Orville Flynn had suspended him. He would not have played either way, no matter whether he had switched to the girls' team or not. If anyone was to blame, it was Orville Flynn, not Gary Whipple. Yes, that loss, if due to Gary's absence, had to be marked against Orville Flynn.

The comfort of Gary's reasoning lasted only a moment. His conclusion that the blame was Orville Flynn's gave Gary pause. Perhaps Gary was indeed at fault, not Orville Flynn. Gary was the one who clowned around on the court. Maybe Orville Flynn just did what he had to do.

Gary shrugged the thought away. It was an uncomfortable one.

By Tuesday night, when Gary stepped onto the court in the Lambert High gym for his warm-up shots, he had the distinct feeling that the roller coaster of his life was going down more often than up.

During the van ride from Madison, he had sat slumped in a window seat staring out at the fading light of the late afternoon, his chin resting on his fist.

And now the anticipation of the game, the roar of the crowd, the dramatic effect of the arc lights bathing the scene—none of these succeeded in overriding the empty feeling that something was not right with the world.

Now even the *thump-thump-thump* of a sure-handed dribbler at work—normally a signal of excitement—seemed not to matter. The *thonk-thonk* of a basketball smacking the backboard, then the rim, before dropping through—the biggest thrill of the game—faded out with little meaning.

Gary was puzzled by the emptiness of things, and he was frowning as he dribbled toward the edge of the keyhole and fired a one-hander toward the basket. His was one of half a dozen shots heading for the basket. As the shot reached the peak of its arch, the crowd of Lambert High fans jammed in the gymnasium suddenly erupted in a roar of a cheer. Gary watched his shot bound off the left side of the rim and fall away.

Then he glanced at the sideline. The Lambert High Hornets, in their purple-and-silver uniforms, were running onto the court. There were twelve of them, the legal limit in the Black Hawk Big Seven Conference.

Five of them were boys.

Chapter Twelve

The Pirates were standing around Monica at the bench. They were moments away from the game's opening tip-off. All heads were turned. All eyes were staring down the court. They were staring down the sidelines, across the scorer's table at the Lambert High bench.

Clearly, the five boys were going to start the game for the Lambert High Hornets. The boys were standing in a semicircle in front of their coach, a short, chunky woman wearing jeans and a plaid shirt. She was speaking. Some of the boys were unconsciously nodding in acknowledgment. At the outer edge of the semicircle, the girls stood and listened.

The Lambert High crowd was rocking the gym with laughter, shouts, and cheers.

Gary turned back to the huddle at the Madison High bench. He glanced at Monica. She was still staring at the Lambert High players. She was sizing up the unexpected lineup her Pirates were going to be facing. The team was different from the one Monica had had in mind when she drafted the Pirates' game plan. Very different—bigger, certainly; better, quite probably. Monica appeared calm, almost casual, as she took the measure of the Hornets. But Gary knew the strategy wheels were whirling inside the coach's head.

He shifted his weight nervously from one foot to the other. The empty feeling of the last two days, the bothersome feeling that things somehow weren't right, was still with him. The feeling, new to him, continued to puzzle him.

The caper was going great. Crazy from the start, the caper was getting crazier with each wild turn of events. Now with Lambert High about to put five boys on the court, the caper was approaching epoch proportions. It was no longer just crazy. It was a circus in a lunatic asylum.

So why wasn't it fun? Why the empty feeling?

Gary looked at Frances. Their eyes met. Frances gave Gary a small smile. She seemed nervous. Gary rolled his eyes at her and managed a grin. As the grin was fading, Gary remembered Frances' initial encounter with number 12 of the Lionel Falls Tigers. Tough, talented Frances had turned into timid, tentative Frances in the face of the boy. The boy had scored. Worse yet, Frances had been humiliated. Was she worried about embarrassment tonight?

Gary glanced at Rita. Rita's gaze was riveted on the cluster of Lambert High Hornets on the other side of the scorer's table. Was she remembering her first encounter with number 12? Rita Cranston's quick feet and quick hands had been reduced to harmless slow motion. Rita had flushed red with embarrassment. True, both of them had bounced back and redeemed themselves. But now there were going to be five boys.

Gary's glance fell on Sharon Richardson. She had

ridden the bench since he joined the team. With Gary on the team, Sharon was watching from the sideline instead of playing on the court.

From Sharon, Gary's thoughts turned to the girls on the Lambert High team. He turned and looked back at them. Five of the seven girls on the edge of the semicircle were going to be watching instead of playing tonight. The boys had knocked them out of their starting roles.

Monica's voice jerked Gary back from his thoughts.

"Hear me!" Monica snapped.

She had turned her back on the Lambert High Hornets. She was facing her players.

She glanced quickly around at the crowd, her expression revealing that she considered the Lambert High fans part of the opponent. In basketball, a supportive crowd was like a sixth player on the court. The cheering fans were worth points. And this crowd, more than most, was a rollicking, noisy, excited bunch. They were going to see something special, and they were loving every minute of it. In these circumstances, they were sure to be a factor.

"Frances, stay back under the basket. You won't be doing much with hook shots from ten feet out tonight. Stay back, and watch for the high pass. Gary and Ruth, send the ball up to her, high—high, understand?"

Gary nodded.

"It'll help a lot if we can score the first goal. It'll set them back on their heels. It'll shut the crowd up. It'll make *our* pace the pace of the game from the outset." Monica paused. She smiled. "That's good coaching, isn't it?—telling you to score."

Her smile seemed to relax the tense faces around her. Maybe there was nothing to worry about. Maybe there was nothing to fear. After all, boys or girls, Lambert's Hornets could only put five players on the court. The Madison High Pirates had five players to match them.

"If we win the tip," Monica continued, "Frances, you head for the basket—like fast, understand?—and be ready for a quick high pass. Quick, I said." She glanced at Gary and Ruth. "Get the ball up there to Frances in the first second, if you can."

A buzzer sounded. The referee, ball in hand, was walking toward the center of the court. Down the court, across the scorer's table, the five boys and seven girls in the purple and silver of the Lambert High Hornets were leaning in, hands clasped, pumping, and shouting, "Let's go."

But Monica was not extending her hands to signal the traditional team handclasp. She was leaning into the semicircle of players. "One other thing, quickly," she said. "On defense, the most devastating thing you can do to an opponent is steal the ball. We need a steal early. It'll rock them back just like a field goal." She looked at Rita. "I want you to steal the ball the first time the Hornets come down the court. The rest of you, tighten the zone around Rita when the ball is in her area so she can go to work. Okay?"

Rita, her teeth clenched tightly, nodded.

The players quickly clasped hands in the center, and the starters turned and ran onto the court—Frances at center, Gary and Ruth at the forwards, Debbie and Rita at the guards.

The Hornets' center, half a head taller than

Frances, grinned at her in a friendly manner and extended his right hand. Frances, surprised, blinked up at him. Then she put out her hand and they shook.

The crowd roared.

Gary wondered if Frances, ever before in her entire basketball career, had been forced to look up to see the face of an opponent on the court.

The referee spun the ball into the air. Frances and the Hornets' center went up. Frances was a good jumper. But so was the Hornets' center. It was no contest. The Hornets' center easily flicked the ball toward the Pirates' goal, away from Gary.

But Rita beat her opponent into the open space and grabbed the ball. The boy had been too casual in his reach for the ball—just a bit, but enough. Rita hugged the ball to her stomach with both hands, protecting the ball against the stabbing hands of the Lambert boy now trying to make up for his lapse.

Frances, having lost the jump and sure the ball was in the Hornets' hands, held her station in the center circle. She looked around for the ball. When she found it in Rita's hands, she turned and raced for the basket. Her moment's delay was too much. The Hornets were surrounding her.

Rita pivoted away from her guard and dribbled forward a couple of steps in front of the retreating Hornets moving back into their defensive positions.

Under the basket, Frances found herself entangled in a web of three Lambert players weaving back and forth through her lane under the basket. Clearly, the Lambert coach knew of Frances Holcott. The Madison team might have a boy playing at one of the forward positions, but the major threat was the big redheaded girl operating under the basket. The three Lambert players made a wall of their moving bodies. Frances was covered at every turn.

Rita rifled a pass down the sideline to Ruth and then advanced toward her.

Ruth looked at Frances, trapped behind a net of waggling arms and jogging legs. She turned and fired the ball back to Rita.

Rita, at twenty feet out, was virtually alone. The Hornets were packing a lot of their defense under the basket, blocking Frances. They were putting a lot of the remainder of their defense on Gary. Rita and the other Pirates, when outside the dangerous range, moved with a freedom rarely seen.

Rita hesitated only a second. Then she set herself and lofted a shot toward the basket.

The ball arched high. It seemed to Gary to hang in the air for a full minute. He ran forward to join Frances in the battle of the boards if the shot went awry. The ball dropped through the nets without touching the rim.

As Monica had predicted, the crowd fell silent. Then a shout from the Madison High fans huddled together at the opposite end of the court broke the quiet.

"Atsa-way!" Gary shouted and shot a fist in the air.

Rita was grinning and accepting a pat on the back from Ruth. She had, in effect, stolen the ball during the Hornets' first possession, as directed by Monica Conway. Then she had put the Pirates on the scoreboard first, also as directed by Monica Conway.

Five somber boys in the purple-and-silver uniforms of the Lambert High Hornets arranged themselves for their first assault on the Madison goal. Gary, backpedaling into his defensive position, could not help grinning at the sight of the serious faces approaching him. Bad enough if Gary had stolen the tip-off. Bad enough if Gary had pumped in the game's first field goal. But a girl—a small girl, at that—had stolen the tip-off. The same girl had scored the first field goal. The Lambert High boys were frowning as they brought the ball down the court.

There was more to their seriousness than facial expressions. The Lambert High boys went to work. Under the basket, the tall center, thanks to his height, was more than a match for Frances. He was not a better player, but he was half a head taller, and he was stronger. Frances battled him every step of the way. But she could not overcome the gift of nature that Frances normally reserved for herself in a basketball game. Rita was easily the master of her opponents. Twice in the first quarter, with the zone defense pulled tight around her, Rita stole the ball out of the hands of a Hornet. But Debbie and Ruth were in deep trouble against opponents who were taller, stronger, and well-equipped with the skills of the game. For Gary, the Hornets, male gender, were no different from dozens of boys he had competed against. He found himself extended to the limits of his abilities. But he was able to function effectively.

At the end of the first quarter the Hornets held a 13–8 lead. Rita's long field goal, a lay-up by Gary, a lay-up by Rita, and a tip-in by Frances comprised the total of points scored by the Pirates in the first eight minutes of play.

Walking off the court toward the bench for the brief intermission, Gary shuddered when he thought how much worse the Pirates' plight might be. The Pirates, for all the fact that they were trailing by five points, had been lucky. Without Rita's steal of the opening tip-off, the Hornets—not the Pirates—might have scored the first field goal. Without Rita's two steals in her zone, the Hornets might have driven to two more field goals. Gary glanced up at the scoreboard. The Pirates were taking a sounder whipping than the numbers in lights indicated. The score could just as easily be 19–6.

At the bench Gary took a towel and wiped the sweat off his face. "Tough going," he said to nobody in particular.

Frances smiled wanly at him.

He smiled back at her. "Hang in there, Red," he said.

His eyes met Pamela's. Pamela was not smiling this time.

"Hear me," Monica said. She spoke the words flatly, in a conversational tone. They carried to the players around her above the din of the boisterous crowd.

Gary leaned closer. He did not want to chance missing a single word. For sure, Monica was going to detail changes in the Pirates' strategy. She could not make Frances six inches taller. She could not endow Ruth and Debbie with the quick, sure hands of Rita. She could not inject a dose of Gary's dribbling skills into any of them. But she could change the strategy.

"Frances, on offense, as long as that big boy is in there, move out around the free-throw line. You'll take him with you. It'll open a lane for Gary—and for you, too, Rita—to go in for lay-ups. If he backs off you in order to stop them, Gary and Rita will feed you for hook shots."

In effect, Monica was converting Frances from a severely hampered offensive weapon into a decoy offering high hopes.

"All of you, take care with your shots. Work until you've got the shot you want, and then take it, and make sure it counts. We're only getting one shot at the bucket with all of that height out there for Lambert."

Monica stopped talking and looked past Frances, down the sideline, past the scorer's table. Gary turned to follow her gaze. The Lambert High coach was approaching.

Without a word of greeting, she told Monica, "If he"—she jerked a thumb in Gary's direction—"goes, they go."

Monica glared daggers at the woman. She said nothing.

After a moment the Lambert High coach shrugged and said, "Okay," and turned and walked back to her team.

"One other thing," Monica said, turning back to her players, as if the interruption had not occurred. "Rita, let's give them a full-court press."

The first minute of the second quarter, with Monica's new tactics in force, wiped the frown off Gary's face and left him grinning again. The sudden movement of Frances out around the free-throw line and the unexpected full-court press by Rita caught the Hornets by surprise. Confusion followed.

In short order the Pirates pumped in three field goals. Gary got the first one, driving under the basket when the Hornets' tall center let Frances lead him out to the free-throw line. Frances got the second field goal when Gary, driving under the basket again, spotted the center turning toward him and flicked the ball back to Frances. She hooked it in. Gary added the third when the center, torn between two assignments, hesitated a second too long.

On defense, Rita got the ball away from a startled guard the first time she showed the full-court press. Later, even when she failed to steal, her tenacious guarding slowed down the Hornets' attack and knocked it off-balance.

But by half time the fact remained that Monica's strategy did not add six inches to Frances' height. It did not give Debbie and Ruth added quickness and ability.

The Pirates headed for the dressing room on the short end of a 24–18 score.

Chapter Thirteen

Walking off the court toward the dressing room for the half-time break, Gary spotted Monica in whispered conversation with Mike Moseley.

He almost wisecracked, "Lovebird talk." Pamela would have giggled. Frances would have smiled. Rita would have frowned. But Gary said nothing. He walked through the door leaving the court and skipped down the stairs to the corridor leading to the boys' dressing room.

When Gary joined the girls in their dressing room, Monica stepped into the center of the floor and signaled for quiet.

"I think we have seen the last of the boys," she said. "Mike just told me that three of them are starters on the boys' team, and the coach is about to have a fit. He okayed their playing the first quarter—not the first half. He didn't want to create a public scene pulling them out. But he's having his say right now during the half time."

Gary, seated on a bench, a towel draped over his shoulder, was breathing heavily. Monica's information explained the funny move on the part of the Lambert High coach at the end of the first quarter.

She had gone out of her way to offer to pull out her boys if Monica would pull out Gary. She needed to pull her five boys off the court. Gary smiled at the thought of her dilemma. He could imagine the words being spoken in some empty corridor right this minute. Relations around the ol' athletic department at Lambert High were going to be a bit strained for some time to come. Especially if the Lambert High boys lost their game to the Pirates.

"But we've still got a ball game on our hands," Monica said, "and we're six points behind."

On the court for the brief warm-up session before the start of the second half, the Lambert High Hornets were again an all-girl team. The boys were nowhere in sight.

Gary, firing a practice shot toward the hoop, then running forward to grab the rebound, spotted Kimberly out of the corner of his eye. She was standing off the end of the court, alone. She was watching him.

Gary raced under the basket, picking off the falling ball with one hand, and swerved his path to dribble toward Kimberly. She quickly turned her head the other way. Gary dribbled past her, heading back toward the center of the court.

Monica signaled from the sideline, and the players joined her at the bench for the last seconds before the start of the second half.

"These girls are nobody's patsies," she said. "But if you play the second half the way you played the first half—with alertness, with intensity—you can make up the six-point deficit and then some."

Frances won the jump and flicked the ball to Gary.

He dribbled forward three paces while Frances raced to the basket. The Pirates passed the ball around the semicircle—Gary to Debbie, Debbie to Rita, Rita to Ruth. At the instant Ruth got her hands on the ball, Frances moved around in front of her guard. Ruth zipped a pass in to Frances. Frances stepped forward and grabbed the ball. And, all in the same movement, she went up, turning, the ball in her right hand, poised for a hook shot. She turned the ball loose. It traveled the inches to the basket and fell through. The deficit was cut to four points.

From there the teams swapped goals. But by the end of the third quarter the Pirates had the lead, 32–31, on Gary's ten-foot jump shot from the corner at the buzzer.

Monica began feeding substitutes into the game— Sharon for Gary, Pamela for Debbie—and Gary spent the fourth quarter watching the game from the bench.

Sitting forward, elbows on knees, chin resting on his fists, staring at the action on the court, Gary concluded that the Pirates—the all-girl version—were smooth, effective, powerful. The all-girl Hornets were not a bad team either. Monica was right: They were nobody's patsies. But the Pirates were outrunning them, outjumping them, outshooting them at every turn. Frances was easily the match in both skills and strength of many a center Gary had seen on boys' teams. She was the master of the game against the Lambert High girl playing center. Rita was a spark plug. Her spectacular plays against the all-boy lineup had not been flukes. Rita was good. The rest of the Pi-

rates—Debbie and Ruth, even Sharon and Pamela—
were no worse than average. There was not a serious
gap in the lineup. Gary reflected that two stars such
as Frances and Rita in a lineup of five had carried
many a basketball team to the heights of the state
tournament.

Gary thought of the state tournament. This team,
the one in front of him now, would be playing in the
tournament. Gary would not. The rule was clear: no
boys on girls' teams, or vice versa, in a state tournament.

The clock ran out on the fourth quarter as Frances,
taking a high pass from Sharon, turned and dunked
the ball in the basket. The final score: Pirates 47,
Hornets 40.

Horse Mueller was having some of the same troubles Frances Holcott had experienced with the Lambert High Hornets' tall center. Horse was not half a
head shorter, but he was shorter by a couple of
inches. And the Hornets' center, a good jumper, made
the difference seem greater. Horse got his nickname
for his strength and not for his ability to jump straight
up in the air. The Hornets' center was having no
trouble controlling the boards at both ends of the
court. If his half time of play in the girls' game had
wearied him, he was doing a good job of hiding the
fact.

But Howie had a hot hand from the corner in the
early going and pumped in four field goals. His point
production kept the Pirates in the running, despite
the tall center's dominance of the boads. The Pirates

finished the first quarter trailing by one point, 15–14.

Gary sat in the bleachers with the crowd—four seats away from Pamela, thanks to careful planning—and watched the Pirates troop off the court toward the bench for the brief intermission. Howie, with nine points on his four field goals and one free throw, showed the excitement of his success. He was breathing heavily but flushed and smiling. Horse bore the burden of his frustrations. His frown was deeper than ever. As he walked to the bench, Horse cast a glance to his left, in the direction of the tall Lambert High center, source of all his troubles.

At the Pirates' bench, the impeccable Orville Flynn awaited the arrival of his players. The coach appeared no more ruffled than if his team had just run up a 30–0 first-quarter lead. If anything ever bothered Orville Flynn, he never let it show.

Gary knew what Orville Flynn would be saying to his players at the bench. To Horse: Move around more. Make the tall center work. He played a half before this game ever started. He's going to get tired. The earlier the better. Make him run out of gas. To Howie: Keep shooting. You're hot. The hot shooter ought to keep shooting. To everyone: Feed Howie because he's hot. Also to everyone: Make sure of your shots. We're not getting a second chance with the tall center grabbing all the rebounds.

The players, toweling off their faces, stood around Orville Flynn. Gary watched the coach's mouth work, the expressionless face turned first to Horse, then to Howie, then scanning all the faces. Behind Orville Flynn stood Mike Moseley, glaring at the players. Mike looked like a tightly wound spring about to break loose. Gary grinned. Mike Moseley had to be the most uptight guy he ever saw.

Mr. Flynn absently patted someone on the bottom and sent the team back onto the court.

There was one other order that Orville Flynn might have given the Pirates in their huddle at the bench. If Gary Whipple had been standing in the circle of players around him, he undoubtedly would have given it. Gary had heard the order many times in similar situations. To Horse: Move out from under the basket. To Gary: In the lane behind Horse, go under for lay-up shots. Gary's lay-up shots would have provided the perfect complement to Howie's hot shooting from the corner. The threat of Gary going under would tear the tall Lambert High center between two assignments, same as in the girls' game. The added work would speed the arrival of his weariness.

Gary sighed at the sight of the players returning to the court. Trailing by one point, they needed Gary Whipple to complete the strategy for a turnaround on the scoreboard. He wondered if they knew it. He was sure they did. No wonder Howie had pleaded with him. No wonder the others were increasingly cool toward him.

On the court, the tall Lambert High center was missing from the lineup.

Gary spotted him on the bench, sitting with a warm-up jacket draped around his shoulders. He thought, More pooped than you were showing, huh, fella? But then Gary had another, less reassuring thought. The big center was being saved for the second half and the stretch run to the finish.

Without the tall center in there, Horse captured control of the boards. Howie stayed hot with his shots from the corner. And the Pirates galloped to a 32–26 lead at half time.

Gary stood up with the rest of the crowd and watched the teams walk off the court for the half-time intermission. He scanned the crowd, looking for Kimberly. He spotted her moving toward the concession stand. He worked his way down the bleacher steps to the floor and moved through the milling crowd toward her.

Coming up behind her, he said, "Since I wasn't able to sit with Pamela, I might as well buy you a Coke."

She started to turn. Then she stopped. He saw her neck stiffen.

"What'll it be?" the concessionaire asked, leaning across the counter.

"A Coke," Kimberly said.

"Two Cokes," Gary announced, pulling out some coins and sliding them across.

The concessionaire produced two Cokes and took the coins.

"You're going to have to turn around sometime," Gary said, "or you're going to look mighty funny walking out of here backwards."

Kimberly turned, gave him an icy glare, and walked away. He followed her to a spot outside the crowd around the concession stand.

"What's wrong with you?" he asked. "Can't you take a joke?"

"It's not a joke," she said.

"I've smiled at Pamela lots of times before."

"It's not that."

Gary grinned. "You never fussed when I used to hug Howie for making a goal," he said.

Kimberly almost smiled.

"And I didn't hug Pamela on the court tonight, did I?" He paused. "Not once," he said. He paused again. "Of course, tonight she didn't score a single field goal."

This time Kimberly did smile.

"Meet me in the lobby in the morning before classes, will you?"

Kimberly took a deep breath and said nothing.

"I promise not to sit with Pamela during the second half."

She still said nothing.

"I won't even sit next to Rita," he said. "I promise."

"Okay, I'll see you in the morning," Kimberly said. "I've got to go now."

She left to join the other cheerleaders forming at the far end of the court. Gary finished his Coke, dropped the cardboad cup in a waste container, and headed back to his seat. He kept a sharp eye out for Pamela, and settled for a seat next to Frances. He did not know the man on the other side.

At the start of the second half the big center was back on the court for the Lambert High Hornets. So was a smallish, quick-moving little guard who trailed Howie like a shadow.

The combination worked for Lambert High, and at the finish the scoreboard read: Hornets 52, Visitors 50.

Gary was standing when the final buzzer sounded.

The Pirates' guards were trying desperately to bring the ball across the center stripe for a final frantic shot. They never got it off. The Lambert High crowd cheered the finish, almost drowning out the buzzer. The Madison fans around Gary were silent.

Gary moved slowly down the row of bleacher seats with the crowd toward the door.

The girls' team's van, with Monica at the wheel, pulled into the darkened parking lot alongside Madison High. A couple of cars at the other end of the lot turned on their lights. They were parents waiting to pick up girls for the ride home. This was Tuesday night. There was no party at the school.

During the thirty-minute drive from Lambert, the van was filled with the laughter of the girls. They relived Rita's steals from the boys. Even Rita was smiling and offering joking comments. They retold the story of the big center's expression when Frances moved out to the free-throw line, clearing a lane for Gary and Rita under the basket. They were a happy team. They had won. No one mentioned the unhappy fate of the boys' team, caught two points behind when the clock ran out, a loser for the second time in three games.

For once, Gary was not a part of the laughter. Usually he was the leader. This time he was not laughing at all. He sat alone, slumped in a corner of the back seat.

When the van rolled to a halt, Gary was the last to step out. He could see girls walking in the darkness toward the headlights of the parked cars. Monica was standing by the door. She always waited to make sure all her girls had a ride home before locking the van and walking to her own car.

"Monica," Gary said tentatively. He could not see her face in the shadows. "I think I need to talk to you."

"Now?" Monica asked. She spoke matter-of-factly. She did not sound surprised. "Right now?"

"Yeah, I think now."

Monica hesitated. Maybe Mike Moseley was meeting her somewhere. Then she locked the van's door and said, "All right, let's go inside to my office."

Chapter Fourteen

They walked around a corner of the gymnasium and Monica unlocked the side door. Inside, she flicked on a light in the corridor running through the basement below the playing court, and they walked to her office. She unlocked the door, turned on the light, walked around her desk, and sat down. Gary stood in front of her desk. She gestured to a chair. He sat down.

For a moment neither of them said anything. Monica picked up a pencil from her desk and rolled it between her fingers, watching him.

Gary was positive that Monica knew what was coming.

"I think I'd better go back to the boys' team," he said finally. Then, after a pause, he added, "If Mr. Flynn will have me."

"Yes," Monica said matter-of-factly, tapping the pencil lightly and watching him.

Yes? What did she mean by that? Finally, Gary repeated her word questioningly. "Yes?"

Monica laid the pencil down and leaned forward. "Yes, I agree with your decision," she said. "I think that is exactly what you should do now—switch back to the boys' team."

Gary did not know whether he should be surprised or not. She had accepted him on the girls' team. So why should she be agreeing with his decision to go back to the boys' team? But she knew every bit as well as Gary—and maybe better—about all of the problems that seemed to be growing on all sides. So why shouldn't she agree with his decision?

Monica smiled at him. "When did you decide this?"

"Well, I've been thinking. . . ."

"Thinking what?"

"This is messing everything up—my being on the girls' team."

Monica smiled again. "It does seem that way, doesn't it?"

"I mean, everybody is playing boys against girls and girls against boys, and all that."

"Yes, it gets confusing."

"But there's more than that."

"Yes?"

"Well, for one thing, the Pirates—I mean, the boys' team—well, they lost over there tonight. They needed me. They would have won if I'd been playing." He stopped. "I don't mean that I'm all that good, but—"

"I understand. And I agree with you."

"The other night, they would've whipped Bennington if I'd been playing. I'm not a starter, I know, but—"

"You're absolutely right."

"Howie and, well, all the rest of them, well, they're getting kind of sore about the whole thing."

"I imagine they are," Monica said. "I saw the game

tonight. I saw the Bennington game. There's no question about it, they need you. As a matter of fact, I don't imagine the Lionel Falls game gave any of the Pirates much comfort. They won it, but only barely."

"That's what I mean."

"As I told you, Gary, I think you are absolutely right in this decision."

Gary was not finished. "There's one other thing, too."

"Yes? What's that?"

"I know that I can't play in the state tournament with the girls' team. Okay, so I can play in the regular season. But I can't play in the tournament. That's one place where they've got us—got me—with a rule that's already on the books."

Monica nodded.

Gary took a deep breath. "I was watching them out there tonight when I was on the bench in the fourth quarter. They're pretty good—all of them—a good team. Maybe good enough to go all the way—win the state championship. I really think so."

"I do, too," Monica said.

"Well, if they're used to playing all season with me at forward, and then they have to go into the tournament without me, well, I—" He broke off his own sentence. "It's just that, well, Sharon is missing all of this playing time, and the team would have to go into the tournament playing a different way from how they've played all season. It's not that I'm so good. . . ." He let the sentence trail off.

"That's true," Monica said. "It would give us a handicap."

Gary looked at Monica. "I want to see them win. I don't want to hurt them. And I think I am—hurting the team."

Monica watched Gary without speaking.

"I think I'm hurting everyone everywhere," he said softly.

For one of the few times in his life, he did not feel like jumping off the railing into the swimming pool at the Holiday Inn, to the delight and amazement of all. He had trouble remembering why he had ever dribbled on his knees or had taken those deep bows. He did not know why he had saluted Horse Mueller in the midst of a game. Why had he started this caper—switched to the girls' team—in the first place? Why? He couldn't remember.

"You keep saying that I'm right," he finally said. "Then what—"

Monica smiled at him again. She was leaning back in her chair now, relaxed. She looked genuinely pleased about something. She picked up the pencil and tapped it lightly on the desk again.

"You mean, then why didn't I fight you when you first announced you wanted to come out for the girls' team? Why didn't I try to talk you out of it? And now, why am I not trying to talk you into staying with the girls' team?"

"Well," Gary said, "yes, I guess so."

"I told you that day in this very office—you remember—that my own personal feelings, my principles, were that full equality of the sexes meant one team: boys and girls on one team, with the best players getting the playing time."

133

Gary nodded.

"Some people are convinced that equality means that the girls are entitled to have a team if the boys are entitled to have a team. I don't agree with that."

"Yes, but—"

Monica waggled the pencil slightly. "Wait a minute," she said. "I'm getting to the point."

Gary grinned slightly.

"When you bobbed up suddenly and said you wanted to play for the girls' team, I was delighted. Oh, I knew it was going to cause a lot of hassle. But it was the perfect opportunity to prove my point. Girls, if they were good enough, could compete with boys. And you, Mr. Gary Whipple, were the perfect character for the role."

Gary nodded slightly. He understood. He was good enough to give the girls a test—a taste of competition against a boy. That was important. Equally important, the boy in the case was Gary Whipple. He had, after all, dribbled on his knees, taken bows, given salutes.

"You came to me," Monica said. "I didn't go to you. It was your idea, not mine. I couldn't have approached you—or any other boy on Mr. Flynn's team—to make the switch. The job of the coach is not to use the players to prove a point, no matter what. But—" she paused and grinned at him "—there you were, asking for the role. Do you understand?"

"Yes."

"Now the time has come to end it, and you are quite right to suggest returning to the boys' team.

You're right when you say that Mr. Flynn's team needs you. They certainly do. You're right when you say you're hurting our chances of going all the way in the state tournament. You are. And"—she lifted her hands and rolled her eyes—"you're certainly correct when you say that things are getting all messed up. Are they ever!"

Gary should have grinned at the sight of Monica's waving arm and rolling eyes. But his face was serious. He was not grinning. The caper, so perfect at the outset, so funny in the unfolding, had turned out not to be funny at all. The boys' team was stumbling and losing because Gary Whipple was missing. The girls' team was heading toward the state tournament at a disadvantage because of Gary Whipple. A funny scene? Yes, it had been, for a while. But now? No, not at all.

"Do you think Mr. Flynn will take me back?" he asked.

"I have no idea," Monica said. "I've not discussed it with him at all."

Gary nodded. He stood up. His eyes were on a level with the two photographs on the wall behind Monica—last year's girls' team, and Monica herself as a player. Gary looked down at her. "You're pretty good," he said.

She smiled up at him. "You're pretty good yourself, Mr. Gary Whipple," she said. "It takes quite a guy to be the only boy on the girls' team. And you're not a bad basketball player, either."

Gary smiled at her, nodded again, and walked out the door.

Walking home in the darkness, his hands stuffed in his pockets against the autumn chill, Gary wondered whether he should call Howie right away. Howie would be pleased with the decision. Howie would spread the word to the other players.

But, no, Howie would have to wait. Orville Flynn should be the first to hear the word from Gary. Probably Orville Flynn already knew—already, by this moment. Monica surely had wasted no time in calling him with the news. But still, Gary figured, Orville Flynn should be the first at the school to hear it straight from Gary.

Gary wondered about Orville Flynn's reaction. He could say, "Welcome back, son." He could give him a big smile and a fatherly hug. But Orville Flynn wouldn't. That wasn't Orville Flynn's style. He might say, "So what? Who needs you?" But he wouldn't. That wasn't Orville Flynn's style either. He might say, "All right, but the suspension begins now." Gary squinted into the darkness as he turned onto his street, and he swallowed hard. He knew there was a real chance Orville Flynn would say exactly that: "The suspension begins now." He hoped Orville Flynn wouldn't say it.

Gary turned his thoughts to Kimberly. She was going to be pleased, for sure. He would tell her when they met in the lobby, right after he saw Orville Flynn. Funny, he thought, that Kimberly hadn't liked the caper from the start. It was hard to figure girls. Kimberly always liked a laugh. But not this time. Well, it was just as well. She would have to get used to doing without laughs at the Pirates' games from now on. Gary Whipple's days of dribbling on his knees were finished.

Howie's face appeared in Gary's mind. It wore the expression Gary had seen when they were sitting together in Howie's Jeep at Lake Jackson. Howie had asked Gary to return to the team. Gary had refused. Howie's expression had not been a pleased one. Now, with the Lambert High loss in the record book, how was Howie going to view Gary's return? How were the others on the team going to take it?

Gary shrugged his shoulders as he skipped up the steps of the front porch and opened the door and stepped in.

"Where's Dad?"

Gary's mother looked up from a magazine and gestured toward the den. "How did it go tonight?" she asked.

"We won, the boys lost," Gary said as he walked through and headed for the den. He peeled off his jacket as he went, dropping it on a chair.

Gary took a deep breath. Telling Monica Conway that he was switching back to the boys' team had been a relief. Asking Orville Flynn if he could return was going to be rough duty. Telling Kimberly was going to be a happy occasion. And he hoped that telling Howie was going to be fun. But best of all was going to be telling his father. He knew exactly what he wanted to say.

Gary's father, seated at a card table laden with papers, poked at a calculator with his forefinger and jotted a figure. Then he looked up at Gary. "Did I hear you say the Pirates lost?"

Gary grinned. "Depends on how you look at it. The girls' team won, the boys' team lost."

"Oh, sorry about that."

"Well, that's sort of what I want to talk to you about."

"Oh?" His father turned in the chair and leaned back.

Gary dropped onto the arm of an overstuffed chair. "I told Monica tonight that I want to switch back to the boys' team," he said. "I'm going to talk to Mr. Flynn in the morning."

"Good," his father said. "I'm glad to hear it." He paused, studying Gary. "What brought about this decision? Was it the loss tonight?"

"In a way, yes," Gary said slowly. "But, well, more than that. . ."

"What?"

Gary grinned at his father. "I finally figured out that other things are more important than a laugh."

Chapter Fifteen

"Frances Holcott wha-a-at?"

"You heard me," Howie said. "She's switching to the boys' team."

Gary and Howie were walking toward the cafeteria for lunch. Around them the corridor was filled with students, milling in both directions. Some were heading away from the cafeteria, having had the first lunch period and now being on their way back to their classes. Others, having the second lunch period, drifted in the same direction as Gary and Howie.

To Gary, the whole scene had turned into a blur. He was speechless.

Gary's interview with Orville Flynn, first thing in the morning, had gone well. He could not have asked for more. Mr. Flynn simply nodded in acknowledgment of Gary's statement, gazed at him, and said, "Very well." That was all. Just "Very well." Orville Flynn might just as easily have been acknowledging that Gary's bout with the flu was over and he was ready to return. Nobody, neither Mr. Flynn nor Gary, made the first mention of the suspension. There was no mention of anything—just "Very well."

Howie, the first player to know, and Kimberly, the next person to know, were pleased to the point of

139

elation. Even Horse Mueller almost smiled when he heard the news.

Smooth as silk, everything was returning to normal.

But now Howie was telling him that Frances was jumping the girls' team to join the boys' team.

"Where did you hear this?"

"It's all over everywhere."

"What do you mean, all over?"

"Everybody knows. I heard it from Hubie and he heard it from Frances herself. Surprised you didn't hear it."

"I can't believe it."

"Well, it's true. She went to Monica Conway this morning and announced her intentions and then went around the corner to Mr. Flynn's office and let him have the grand news."

"Must've been after I was in there," Gary mumbled to himself. He wondered how Monica Conway's principles of equality faced up to the fact that her center—the star of the team—was switching to the boys' team. Probably she did not smile. He wondered how Mr. Flynn had reacted. Calm as ever, for sure.

"She told Hubie that after playing against those five boys at Lambert last night, including that big center, she figured she could hack it on the boys' team—and that the boys' team is the real team."

Gary grimaced at Howie's statement. He felt a pang of guilt. He had crippled the boys' team by quitting. He had hampered the girls' team by joining them. Now he had moved to set things straight, only to find he had set the stage for more trouble. The girls' team was being crippled. The boys' team was headed for a mess.

The two turned from the corridor into the cafeteria. Across the way they saw Kimberly and another cheerleader and Barbara, along with Hubie and Horse, seated at a table. They waved, picking up their trays and moved into the food line.

As they approached the table with their food, they heard the chatter at the other table: Frances Holcott was switching to the boys' team.

"Oh, brother," Gary mumbled to himself.

He was hardly seated before Horse snarled, "You really started something with your little gag."

Behind Horse, Mike Moseley walked by. Gary lowered his eyes and concentrated on finding a bite of food on the tray in front of him.

"Gary didn't tell her to do it," Kimberly said to Horse.

"It's sort of what they call a precedent having been set," Horse stated.

"Horse is worried that Frances can beat him out," Howie joked.

Gary glared at Howie. He and his friend had shared a lot of laughs. This was one laugh they could do without. Horse, apparently in agreement with Gary's thought, did not dignify Howie's statement with an answer.

"You know," Hubie said softly, "there is one person who can talk her out of it."

"Oh?" Gary said between bites.

"You."

"You know, of course," Monica Conway said quietly, "there *is* one person who can talk her out of it."

Gary, seated across the desk from her in Monica's small office, was already late for his first practice back with the boys' team. But he knew what Monica Conway had in mind when she motioned him into her office. He couldn't refuse the summons. He didn't hesitate. He walked past the dressing-room door and into her office.

"Let me guess," Gary said. He didn't relish the prospect of trying to talk Frances Holcott out of making the switch. Turning people away from crazy stunts was not exactly what Gary Whipple was noted for. Talk about treading new ground! But he knew that both Hubie and Monica Conway were quite right. He *was* the only one for the job. "Is it me?" he asked.

Monica didn't smile. "You may think this sounds funny coming from me," she said, "but Frances must not switch—no matter what my personal principles—for the very same reasons that it was right for you to return to the boys' team at this time."

Gary nodded. He understood.

"Frances has hopes of a college scholarship. I don't doubt she can get one. She has dreams of a professional career. She's got good prospects. She says she is convinced that succeeding on a boys' team will help her. In that she is wrong."

"Well, you've talked to her," Gary said tentatively. Maybe, after all, it wouldn't be necessary for him to make the pitch. He hoped so. "You've told her all this."

"She's being a bit stubborn about the whole thing."

"She's a redhead," Gary said, speaking more to himself than to Monica.

Monica ignored Gary's remark. "Frances is helping neither herself nor the boys' team nor the girls' team with this sort of move," she said. "She is hurting them all—herself, the boys' team, the girls' team."

Gary sighed. Yes, he knew all about who was going to get hurt. Sometimes a good caper had a way of getting out of hand, a long way out of hand. "I'll try," he said.

"Good," Monica said abruptly. "She's in the girls' dressing room now, dressing for practice. I'll go in and see if she's dressed. Then you can go in."

"Hi, Red."

"Hi, Gary."

Frances was sitting on a bench in front of a row of lockers. She was waiting for him. Gary sat on a bench opposite her in the empty dressing room.

He grinned at her. "This is kind of silly, isn't it?"

"What do you mean, silly?"

"Me, of all people, being sent in here to talk you out of this stunt."

"It's not a stunt."

"C'mon," Gary said, still grinning at her.

Frances returned the grin. Then she said, "I told Monica that I'd listen to you."

Gary nodded. He let his grin fade away. He took a deep breath. He looked her in the eye. "Red," he said, "you're not going to do this thing."

"Yes, I am. If you can switch, I can switch. And I've got better reasons than you had. With you, it was a joke, just a gag. With me, well, I know that I can play the game with the boys."

"That's just the point."

143

"What's just the point?"

"You're too good."

"Too good?"

Gary shrugged his shoulders. Then he grinned at her again. "I can't believe that I'm saying these things, trying to talk you out of it," he said. "The whole caper sounds like too much fun."

"Then don't try to talk me out of it," she said. "And it's not a caper."

"Let's back up," Gary said. "I said you were too good to be doing this."

"Too good?"

"Right. Now we're getting back on the track."

"I'm getting mixed up. What are you saying?"

Gary rolled his eyes. "First you confuse 'em," he said. "It never fails."

Frances stared at Gary without speaking.

"Red," he said, "if this were Pamela or someone off the bench, everyone probably would say what they said when I switched—okay, so what, let her go. But you're Frances Holcott."

She stiffened a little. "I know who I am," she said.

"Good. That helps. Do you know what you're doing to the girls' team when you leave? Do you know what you're doing to your teammates? It's a team that might win the state championship—if you're on the team. It's a team that will fold—if you're not on the team. Those girls—Rita and Ruth and Debbie, all of 'em—have worked too hard to have this happen to them. And all because you've done the wrong thing—deserted them. They deserve better."

Frances said nothing. She seemed to squirm a bit. Gary had the feeling he had touched a sensitive point.

"Do you know what you're doing to the boys' team the moment you join? The same thing I was doing to the girls' team, that's what: disrupting things, hampering the team, reducing the chances of going into the state tournament with good odds of winning. I finally realized what I was doing, and that's when I switched back."

Again, Frances seemed to squirm a bit.

"Red, when I switched, it was for laughs. You know me, good ol' Gary Whipple, a laugh a minute. Well, I got my laughs, and I left. But you're not doing it for laughs. You're dead serious. You're not going to get a few laughs and then go away. You want to stay. I made enough trouble. But you're going to make more."

The next words seemed to stop in Gary's throat. But he took a deep breath and got them out. "Red," he said, "I regret what I did." He managed a smile and added, "If you ever tell anyone that I admitted that, I will deny it." She smiled at him. He continued, "I regret it because I hurt my team—the boys' team—and contributed to their losing two games. I regret it because now I think I harmed the girls' team, a team of girls who deserve better."

He leaned back against a locker and let the words sink in. Frances was staring at the floor between them.

"If you go through with this," he said finally, "you will have the same regrets, believe me."

After a moment Frances gave a barely perceptible

nod. Then she looked up at Gary and nodded again.

"Yes," she said softly.

"Yes, what?"

Frances smiled slightly. "Yes, I can see that you are right."

Gary grinned at her.

Most of the players were dressed for practice when Gary walked into the boys' dressing room.

"Hey, what are all you guys doing in my dressing room?" he called out. "I'm used to having privacy in my dressing room, with the rest of the team changing in some room down the hall."

Horse looked up with a snort. Howie opened his arms wide and proclaimed, "The prodigal son returns. All hail." Hubie and a couple of others grinned and applauded.

"Please, please," Gary pleaded in mock modesty.

"You're late." Horse said. "It figures."

"Yeah," Howie chimed in. "Hurry and get dressed. We're all going to go upstairs and watch Frances tie Horse in knots under the basket."

Horse glowered at Howie.

"Frances who?" Gary asked, a blank expression on his face.

A few of the players laughed.

"Oh, that Frances," Gary said. "Haven't you heard the latest? She's staying with the girls' team."

Orville Flynn turned and stared at Gary.

Chapter Sixteen

By the hour of Gary's announcement in the dressing room, the students were leaving Madison High and heading home, spreading a sensational story that was no longer true: Frances Holcott was switching from the girls' team to the boys' team. The word of Frances' reversal had no chance of catching up with the original version and correcting it. The Madison High grapevine had been dismantled for the night.

So when Roy Marsh appeared at Madison High early on Thursday morning, the students working in the administration office figured they knew the reason. The president of the Black Hawk Big Seven Conference had come to talk about the new crisis. He was there to discuss the latest problem emanating from Madison High. The Gary Whipple problem was solved. Now there was the Frances Holcott problem.

A few minutes later, when Orville Flynn and Monica Conway appeared in the administration office and walked through to George Gordon's office, the conclusions were confirmed.

The door to George Gordon's office closed behind the two coaches. The students working in the administration office went back to their tasks, checking attendance records, filing, answering the telephone. And the word of the closed-door meeting began to seep out of the administration office and into the corridors of Madison High.

Gary was puzzled. What was there for Roy Marsh and the principal and the two coaches to discuss? Already the story of Frances' change of mind was spreading through the corridors and classrooms. Surely Roy Marsh knew. Surely he had been called immediately when Frances announced to Monica that she intended to switch to the boys' team. Equally certainly, Gary figured, he had been told immediately when Frances changed her mind. So why was Roy Marsh meeting with Orville Flynn and Monica Conway and George Gordon?

Then the puzzlement gave way to a feeling of alarm. The meeting could only mean bad news. With Gary back on the boys' team, and with Frances firmly settled on remaining with the girls' team, there was no problem to discuss. So what was left? Gary did not like the answer his brain provided: punishment, a penalty for all the hassle.

Could the conference declare him ineligible? He had quit the boys' team for the girls' team. Could the conference refuse to let him switch back? It was a possibility. There had to be a limit to switching back and forth. Maybe Roy Marsh felt some punishment—ineligibility—was necessary to discourage some other Gary Whipple in the future from wreaking similar havoc. Undoubtedly ineligibility for Gary Whipple would serve as an effective deterrent.

No, no, surely not, Gary told himself. But he could not shake his frown.

Gary did not have to wonder and worry for long. During the second period he was summoned from a study hall by a messenger from the administrative office. Gary's presence was required in the principal's office.

Walking down the corridor, Gary asked the girl who had delivered the message, "What's up?"

"Don't ask me," she said with a shrug. "I don't know."

They arrived at the administration building. Walking through the reception area toward the principal's private office, Gary found all eyes on him. He raised his eyebrows and grinned back at the questioning stares.

Stepping through the door into George Gordon's office, Gary saw Frances seated on a couch next to Monica.

"Hi, Red," he said.

She smiled at him.

Across from Monica and Frances, Orville Flynn was seated on a chair. On the chair next to Orville Flynn was a man Gary recognized from newspaper photographs as Roy Marsh. George Gordon was seated behind his desk.

Nobody looked happy.

"Have a seat, Gary," Mr. Gordon said.

Gary sat down on a metal folding chair, the last seat in the office. With the six of them there, the office seemed crowded.

George Gordon gestured slightly and Orville Flynn got to his feet and closed the office door and sat back down.

Mr. Gordon said, "Gary, this is Coach Marsh, the

president of the Black Hawk Big Seven Conference."

Gary and the coach nodded at each other. Gary smiled slightly. Roy Marsh did not smile.

The room was silent for almost a full minute. Nobody seemed to know who was supposed to say what. Gary felt again a sense of alarm. Finally Mr. Gordon, scratching the back of his head and appearing decidedly uncomfortable, said, "Monica, why don't you. . ." He let the sentence trail off to nothing.

Monica took a deep breath. Then she said, "Now that things are back to normal—"

Roy Marsh leaned forward and interrupted her. "If I may, Monica," he said.

"Yes?"

"Before we go on, I'd like assurances from both of these students . . . to hear it from their own mouths . . . that their decisions to stay with their own teams are, uh, definite and permanent." He glanced from Monica to Gary and then glanced at Frances. "That is one of the reasons that I suggested we have them sit in on this meeting."

In the moment of silence that followed, Gary realized that everyone was waiting for his answer first. He nodded.

Frances said, "Yes."

"Thank you," Coach Marsh said solemnly. He paused. "The other reason that I asked to have you in the meeting is so you will understand fully the difficulties that you"—he nodded in the direction of Gary—"have caused, and the difficulties that you"—he nodded at Frances—"came very close to causing."

For Gary, the admonition brought a sense of relief. The meeting did not seem like a session convened to declare him ineligible. First, there was the presence of Frances. She never made the switch. She had disrupted nothing. So why was she sitting here in the meeting? Not just to hear about Gary being declared ineligible. Then there had been Monica's abbreviated opening remark. Her "back to normal" gave Gary hope. And now Roy Marsh seemed to be saying that everything was behind them and was going to stay there. The episode was over. The caper was done. Roy Marsh had asked only for promises that this was, indeed, the case. Now he had his promises.

"Yes," Monica said, preparing to begin again. "Now that everything is back to normal, we've been able to work out settlements with the teams involved."

Gary's eyebrow went up slightly. So that was it: the angry women who saw their teams go down to defeat before a team playing a boy had to be placated somehow. Then Gary frowned. He hoped that Monica was not going to say that the Pirates were being forced to forfeit the three games he had helped them win. Already the boys' team had lost two games in his absence. They just might have won the games if he had been available for action. That was penalty enough for Gary. He did not want to think that the girls' team was going to be ruled a loser in one, two, or three games because he had played.

Gary looked at Roy Marsh. The president of the conference was bound to have a big voice in any decision. He would be the mediator, the judge, the jury. Roy Marsh did not appear to Gary at this moment to be in a very sympathetic mood.

Frances, too, was frowning.

Monica seemed to sense their concern. "It's not bad news," she said.

"We didn't really have a problem with the Lambert High game," she said. "Coach Grayson agreed"—here Monica almost smiled—"that playing five boys the entire first half sort of took the wind out of any complaint about our having a boy on the court. And"—she glanced at Orville Flynn—"the Lambert High boys' team victory over our Pirates eliminated any cause for complaint by the boys' coach, who might have felt we forced a severe handicap on his team."

Gary was breathing easier.

"The Lionel Falls Tigers played one boy in their lineup—same as we were playing—and Coach Andrews and I have decided to call it even. The score will stand. Coach Boyd's team—the boys—lost, and he might have complained about having one of his key players worn out in the girls' game. But, after all, he agreed to the use of the boy, so that's that.

"The game with the Bennington Falcons is another matter."

Gary remembered the fury of the coach, pointing a finger at him and shrieking, "Is—that—a—boy?" She had been one angry woman.

"We will replay the game," Monica said. "Coach Mansfield was demanding a forfeiture, as you know. Perhaps her argument has a point. But while Gary may have amounted to an unfair advantage for the Pirates, there is no way to prove it. Sharon might have done as well as Gary. We might have won by the same score if Gary had not played. And anyway, there is no conference rule covering the matter. We finally agreed in all fairness to replay the game."

Monica looked at Roy Marsh. "Coach Marsh was a great help in settling things," she said.

Roy Marsh nodded at her in acknowledgment.

Finished, Monica leaned back.

Gary looked around the room. Was the meeting at an end? No, apparently not. Nobody was moving.

Orville Flynn, who had remained silent throughout, shifted in his seat, and spoke up.

"Gary, you were quite helpful in pointing out to Frances the harm she would be doing herself and everyone else if she switched to the boys' team." Mr. Flynn was speaking slowly, choosing his words carefully. "And now both of you can be quite helpful." He paused and cleared his throat. "What I am saying is this: We hope that no one else is considering a switch."

In spite of himself, Gary grinned. All around him, four adults almost visibly flinched.

Two faces flashed through Gary's mind. One was Howie's. Howie loved a gag almost as much as Gary. The other was the stern-jawed countenance of Rita Cranston. She had the skills to play for any team.

The room was silent, obviously awaiting an answer.

Gary knew the answer. Howie would not leave the boys' team. Rita would not leave the girls' team.

"I don't think it will happen," Gary said. "After all—"

"After all," Monica interrupted, "there is only one Gary Whipple. "

Frances looked at Gary and grinned.

Gary looked at the ceiling.

Chapter Seventeen

By game time the next night, everything did indeed seem back to normal.

Frances Holcott was in the lineup in the girls' game. She poured through twenty-eight points, most of them with her deadly hook shot, leading the Pirates to a 47–33 thrashing of the Mount Holly Raiderettes.

In advance of the boys' game, Gary Whipple was on the court taking his warm-up shots. He was back with the boys.

He grinned when somebody in the crowd called out, "Hey, who's the new girl wearing number 11?" But he was careful not to turn and look in the direction of the shout. The grin on his face lasted only a second. He set himself and fired the ball at the basket.

Normal, too, was the unruffled expression on Mr. Flynn's face. He stood calmly at the sideline watching his players weave and dribble and shoot. With a slight turn of his head, he sized up the Mount Holly Raiders at the other end of the court.

Gary stepped over in front of Howie and caught a loose ball on the bounce. He dribbled in place for a moment, then drove for the basket and laid the ball in. Somebody in the crowd shouted, "Look at that girl go!" This time, Gary did not allow himself even a quick grin. Eyes down, he turned and returned to the outside to join the warm-ups.

The days of Gary Whipple's clowning on the basketball court were gone forever. He had resolved that never again would the laughter drown out the cheers because of Gary Whipple. He had made the silent resolution the moment Mr. Flynn took him back on the team.

For a moment, Gary had considered telling Mr. Flynn about his resolution. It would amount to a promise. But Mr. Flynn asked for no promise. And Gary, on second thought, figured that Mr. Flynn wanted no promise. Mr. Flynn wanted performance. So Gary decided to deliver performance instead of promise. Not even Howie knew of Gary's firm resolve.

A whistle signaled the players to their benches for the final moments before the opening tip-off.

Gary turned and seated himself on the bench while the five starters moved onto the court.

Staring at the scene on the court in front of him, Gary unconsciously began measuring the Mount Holly Raiders. The Raiders, in their red-and-black uniforms, always were tough competition for the Pirates. They, like the Pirates, had a long winning tradition in basketball. Invariably, they had the height, the muscle, the speed, and the skill of a powerhouse team. And also like the Pirates, the Raiders were a well-coached team. They were undefeated in this young season, and they appeared determined to remain that way.

The Madison High crowd was silent as the referee stepped between the two centers. This was an important game for their Pirates, coming after a heart-breaking loss to the Lambert High Hornets. The time for jocular shouts about "the girl wearing number 11" had passed. This was the moment for serious business for the Madison High fans and their Pirates.

Horse won the tip, outjumping the heavy-footed Mount Holly center. The crowd broke the silence with a roar. Horse flicked the ball to Raymo Bailey.

Raymo dribbled twice, waving an arm to position his teammates for the drive to the basket. He fired a pass down the sidelines to Howie. Horse was moving into position in front of the basket. The big Mount Holly center was tracking him. Howie sent a high pass to Horse, who was coming around in front of the Mount Holly center. Immediately, Howie broke for the basket in a path leading behind both Horse and the Mount Holly center. Horse took in the pass above his head, brought the ball down, dribbled once as he turned, and started to go up. With the Mount Holly center going up with him, Horse dropped off the ball to Howie racing under the basket. Before the Mount Holly center knew what had happened, Howie went up and laid the ball on the rim. The ball circled lazily halfway around the rim. Then it dropped through.

The scoreboard flashed: Pirates 2, Visitors 0.

All around the gym, the Madison High fans were on their feet cheering.

On the bench, Gary clapped his hands and then put them to his mouth, forming a megaphone, and shouted, "Hey-hey, attaway!"

From there the two teams swapped goals in a furious sequence of charges up and down the court. That the Mount Holly Raiders were undefeated was no fluke. They had speed and quickness at the guard positions. They had deadeye shooting from the forward positions. Their center, a bit on the slow side, knew how to make up for his shortcoming. He was strong, had a good eye for the basket, and sure hands when rebounding. The Raiders were a match for the Pirates, no question.

With the score 14–13 in favor of the Pirates in the early minutes of the second quarter, Gary began glancing down the bench at Orville Flynn. The Pirates' starting five had played every second of the game so far. They were showing the signs of wear. During the brief intermission between quarters, all five of them had been puffing heavily as they toweled off the streams of perspiration. The Mount Holly coach was already slipping substitutes into the lineup. He was giving his starters a breather. But Orville Flynn let the intermission come and go with the first five all remaining on the court.

Gary was unable to catch Orville Flynn's eye. If the veteran coach was concerned about the nip-and-tuck nature of the game—a game that might easily be decided by a single point—he did not show it. If he sensed the troubling signs of weariness on the part of his starters, he did not show it. He sat on the bench, legs crossed, hands clasped around a knee, and watched the game with his usual expression—a bland stare that looked almost bored.

Gary was frowning as he returned his attention to

the game. The Pirates were leading 17–15. The Raiders had the ball. One of their guards, the smaller one with the long, straight, floppy black hair, was dribbling toward the center stripe. Howie thrust out a hand, reaching for the ball. The little guard turned and dribbled away from Howie, crossing the center stripe. He passed to a forward in the corner.

For Gary, the scene on the court blurred. Had Orville Flynn accepted Gary back on the team only to let him ride the bench? Clearly the situation on the court called for Gary coming off the bench to give Howie or maybe Raymo a few minutes of rest. The furious pace of the game was taking a heavy toll. But here Gary sat. Had Orville Flynn decided that, yes, the suspension remained in force?

Gary wished he had told Mr. Flynn of his resolution. No more gags, honest. No more clowning, ever. Really. Maybe Mr. Flynn had expected a promise of good behavior from Gary. Maybe he had wanted a promise. But he had got none. So now the suspension remained in force. Nobody had said so. Nobody had said anything. Maybe Mr. Flynn felt he did not need to say anything.

A shout of alarm from the crowd brought the court back into focus for Gary. The Raiders, loading their attack to one side of the court, had succeeded in pulling the Pirates' defense out of position. Now the big center was between Horse and the basket. And behind the big center, the little floppy-haired guard dribbled through with the speed of a bullet coming out of a rifle barrel. He flicked the ball upward with a twist. The ball skittered along the backboard and dropped into the net.

The score was tied again—Raiders 17, Pirates 17.

"Thompson! Hubie Thompson!"

Mike Moseley's voice carried down the length of the bench above the shouts of the crowd.

The Raiders had just stolen the ball from Raymo in a sudden double-teaming assault. With two quick passes, they put the ball in the hands of the big center. The center, faking left and turning right, left Horse behind and laid in the ball for a 19–17 Mount Holly lead.

Hubie shucked his warm-up jacket and leaped to his feet.

"In for Leon," Moseley shouted.

Hubie was going in at guard, substituting for Leon Bowman.

Gary looked up and caught Hubie's eyes for a second. Then Hubie headed quickly to the scorer's table to check in. Gary, his elbows on his knees, returned his gaze to the floor.

"Whipple! In for Fenton!"

Gary heard Mike Moseley's voice. He thought he must be imagining things.

"C'mon, Whipple. In for Fenton."

Gary jumped to his feet and dropped his warm-up jacket on the bench. He looked down the bench, seeking Mike Moseley's face. He wanted confirmation. But Moseley was seated next to Mr. Flynn, his shoulders hunched forward, his head leaning in, listening to something Mr. Flynn was saying. They had ordered the substitutions. Now they were charting the strategy for the next few minutes.

Gary ran to the scorer's table. He mumbled,

"Whipple for Fenton," and ran onto the court, waving the winded and perspiring Howie to the bench.

The crowd let out a roar. Gary Whipple, who dribbled on his knees, saluted, took deep bows, was back. They loved it.

The Raiders settled back into their defensive positions. The back-to-back field goals had rocketed them into the lead. Now they were ready to try for another turnover—a steal, a pass interception, a fumble recovery—and another goal.

Hubie took the pass inbounds and turned and began dribbling down the court, heading for the center stripe.

Gary dropped back into his forward position, watching the direction of Hubie's progress and taking the measure of the Mount Holly defenders around him.

As he moved around, awaiting the end of the several seconds it was taking Hubie to arrive and set up the Pirates' attack, Gary sensed a turning point in the game. This was one of those moments—every game had several of them—when the irresistible force of the offense met the immovable object of the defense. Something had to give. Something always did give. One team or the other was going to prevail. The sum of those confrontations was what, in the end, spelled victory for one team and defeat for another. This was one of those moments. Gary could feel it.

Gary was not the only one sensing the importance of the moment. Hubie's face, grim and creased with the frown of concentration, showed that he understood the significance of the play he was setting up. The huddled conversation between Orville Flynn and

Mike Moseley on the bench had been evidence that the coaches knew a moment of importance was at hand. All around Gary, his teammates showed that they felt the electricity of the moment. Raymo, obviously tiring, was nevertheless alert and brisk in his movements. Horse, fighting a tough battle under the boards with the big Mount Holly center, was more intense than ever.

The crowd, too, seemed to know. They were quiet, deathly quiet, as Hubie approached the center stripe.

Hubie dribbled across the center stripe and fired a pass across to his partner at guard, who zipped the ball to Raymo at forward. The Mount Holly zone defense turned and flowed in the direction of the ball with each pass. In and out of the corridor in front of the basket, Horse and the big Mount Holly center muscled each other for position. Raymo shot the ball back to Hubie. Hubie sent the ball down the sideline to Gary in the corner.

Through it all, the Mount Holly defense, swaying in the direction of the ball, seemed flawless, formidable, unbreakable.

Gary faked the start of a drive for the basket. Then he flicked the ball back to Hubie. Hubie dribbled in place for a moment, staring at the Mount Holly defender opposite him. Gary circled around his defender and broke into the clear. Hubie rifled a pass into the open space. Gary grabbed the ball. He turned. He dribbled. He started to go in for a lay-up.

Suddenly he saw nothing but a red shirt with black trim. The big Mount Holly center was hovering over him, blocking his path.

Gary stopped the dribble. He tightened his grip on

the ball. He pivoted on one foot, turning his back to the Mount Holly center. He found himself staring into the face of Horse Mueller. What was Horse doing there? Gary glanced around quickly. Somehow—how?—Gary had wound up between the two centers—separating them—in the lane in front of the basket. And he was holding the ball in his hands.

Gary presented the ball to Horse.

Horse, startled, took it. Gary retreated slightly, taking care not to foul, and tightened his screen in front of the big Mount Holly center. Horse had a clear shot to the basket over Gary and the Mount Holly center.

The crowd roared with laughter. Horse's startled expression had been visible to many of the fans. It certainly was visible to Gary, and he had almost laughed at the sight himself. Gary could imagine how the whole scene looked from the bleachers: formal, stilted, dignified presentation of the ball, perhaps accompanied by the remark, "Here, ol' boy, have a go at it." Gary could imagine, too, how the scene looked from the bench: a Gary Whipple gag.

Horse recovered from his surprise and pumped the ball into the basket easily.

The cheers of the crowd drowned out the laughter.

By that time, Gary was looking at the bench. He was frantic. He wanted to shout, "It wasn't a gag, it wasn't a gag." But he wouldn't have been heard above the roar of the crowd anyway. The Madison High fans knew that their Pirates had prevailed at the turning point. The roar from the bleachers was deafening.

The scene at the bench told Gary nothing. The players were on their feet cheering. That was natural enough. Mr. Flynn was seated, unmoving, presumably neither surprised nor excited about what had happened, as if he had designed the play. That was normal for Mr. Flynn. Mike Moseley was on his feet, shooting a fist into the air the way he always did when the Pirates scored a big goal. That was normal. Everything was normal.

Gary took a deep breath. Nobody was waving him from the court, pulling him out of the game for staging another Gary Whipple clown stunt.

He turned his gaze from the bench and faced Horse Mueller. He spoke before he thought. "No," he said, "I am not going to salute you this time."

Horse blinked at him.

The Raiders were bringing the ball back into play, and Gary backed up into a defense position.

In the end the score was 58–52, and the victory belonged to the Pirates. The Raiders, tough as they were, never reclaimed the lead.

Gary, filling in for Howie at times and for Raymo at other times, finished the game with seven points. Horse, having mastered the big Mount Holly center in the second half, was the Pirates' high scorer with twenty-one points.

The Pirates' dressing room was a wild melee— cheers, shouts, whistles—with no one in a hurry to peel off their uniforms and head for the showers. They were a team that had lost two of the last three games. But now, tonight, they had knocked off the undefeated Mount Holly Raiders. They were on the track and they were rolling. They knew it, and they were enjoying it.

Even Orville Flynn was smiling, allowing himself to be recognized as pleased and satisfied, as he circled the room with a good word for each player.

Mike Moseley approached Gary. "Nice game," he said. "That was a good play," he added, apparently feeling he did not have to identify the play he meant.

Gary grinned. "Thanks," he said.

"I would have sworn for a minute there that you were going to salute or take a bow or something like that," Moseley said. He was staring hard at Gary, as if he could not believe that Gary let the incident pass without a stunt. "I would've bet on it," he said.

Gary kept grinning at Moseley and said nothing.

Moseley finally nodded and walked on to another player.

Orville Flynn appeared in front of Gary. He stood there a moment without speaking. The room around them grew quiet. Gary wished someone would shout, cheer, whistle—anything. The silence was terrible.

"Good game, Gary," Mr. Flynn said. "You played well."

Gary, without cracking a smile, returned Mr. Flynn's gaze and said, "Thank you, sir."

For some reason the room erupted in gales of laughter.